Peregrine has been on the run most of his life. His ability to heal makes him a target, and some people will go to any lengths to get their hands on him. But as long as he doesn't heal anyone, his magic can't be used to locate him. He's safe in Rosewood, and for the first time in his twenty-nine years, he's able to make friends.

Jarvis is dull. He's not athletic or popular like his siblings, and he's always been aware of that. Even his job at the coffee shop is boring, but he enjoys it, and it allows him to watch the people he wishes he could be friends with, including the newcomer, Peregrine.

Peregrine doesn't understand why he's intrigued by Jarvis until they get close and they realize they're mates. It's not just that, though. No matter how ordinary Jarvis thinks he is, he's anything but, and Peregrine falls for the man he is, not for the bond between them.

When Jarvis is hurt, Peregrine doesn't think twice about helping him. He can't heal him, but he can take his pain away, even though it means the people who are after him will find him. Peregrine has to run again so he can keep Jarvis and the pack safe, but Jarvis is stubborn and follows him.

Will they be able to run fast enough that the people trying to capture Peregrine won't get their hands on him? Or will Peregrine lose everything he never allowed himself to wish for right after he found it?

Not Ordinary
Copyright © 2021 Catherine Lievens
ISBN: 978-1-4874-3285-0
Cover art by Angela Waters

Published by eXtasy Books Inc or
Devine Destinies, an imprint of eXtasy Books Inc

Look for us online at:
www.eXtasybooks.com or www.devinedestinies.com

Not Ordinary
Legendary Shifters 6

By

Catherine Lievens

CHAPTER ONE

Peregrine peeked out of his bedroom. He could smell the delicious scents of coffee and bacon, and he yearned to go to the kitchen and have breakfast. He could hear Toby and Cam were still in the house, though, which was why he hadn't headed that way. He knew they'd want to talk to him and try to be his friend, and while he understood why and was grateful, he couldn't allow that to happen. The last thing he needed was to want to stay here in Rosewood.

Peregrine had never stayed anywhere for any length of time. He couldn't afford to, not when he was still in danger. He'd been hunted all his life, and he would continue being hunted until he died. He'd accepted that a long time ago, and while he didn't like it, by now, he knew how to make it easier.

Not having friends made it easy. Not having anyone to leave behind, anyone to put in danger, made it easy.

But Peregrine was sick of it.

He left his bedroom, but instead of going to the kitchen, he turned the other way and headed toward the back door and the forest. Ever since he'd arrived in Rosewood, he'd been spending as much time as possible there. Sometimes he shifted and slept in a tree. Sometimes he just walked around, relieved that he knew he was safe and that nothing would happen to him. He was still vigilant, but he couldn't deny his life was easier now that he was in Rosewood.

It wouldn't last long. It never did. The few times he'd stayed with people, everything had been fine in the beginning, but then things had changed. Someone got sick, and

1

they begged Peregrine to heal them. Peregrine couldn't say no. No matter how much he wanted to, he was a caladrius shifter, with everything that entailed. He had the ability to heal people, and he truly wanted to help. He hated that it was at the sacrifice of his own safety and happiness, but that had never stopped him.

He didn't know how long it would be before the pack asked him to heal someone. They had two unicorn shifters, and at least one of them was studying to be a healer. That was good, and it meant that Peregrine might not be called to help for a while. If he didn't heal, the people looking for him wouldn't be able to find him.

That was what they looked for. They had a way to follow the magic he used to heal, and they always found him. The only times they hadn't was when he hadn't told anyone what he was and hadn't healed anyone. It was tempting to do just that here in Rosewood, and Peregrine hoped the alpha wouldn't ask him to heal anyone. He'd promised that wouldn't be the case, but Peregrine had heard too many promises. If it came to it, Peregrine would have to run.

But in the meantime, no one knew he was here. No one knew who he was or *what* he was. That meant he didn't have to stay in pack territory. Several people had already asked him if he wanted to go into town, but so far, he'd said no. He'd stuck to the forest, too scared of what could happen. He was still frightened, but for once, he wanted to live. He wanted to feel like he was a normal person, at least for a few hours. He couldn't be sure what would happen tomorrow or the day after that, or even in the next hour. What he could be sure of was how he behaved, and he'd had enough of being locked inside. Even though he'd been the one to lock himself up, he was bored, and he wanted more.

He was already outside. Instead of going back into the house and telling Cam what he was doing, he looked around and headed to the road. The Rosewood pack was small, and it consisted of only a handful of houses clustered together with a big fire pit in the middle. The fact that there were so many rare shifters living here was stunning, and it made Peregrine feel like maybe he'd found a home.

He pushed that thought away as he walked down the road. No matter how much he wanted to find a place where he belonged and where he could stay, he knew better than to allow himself to believe that. It was too dangerous. What would happen if someone found out what he was? Then he would have to run, and he would lose it. It was best for him not to think of Rosewood as a home, not when he already knew what the future held for him. It didn't take a seer to know. He'd allowed himself to hope too many times, and every single time, that hope had been squashed. He was done with hope, and he'd decided to focus on the present. It was the only thing he could do.

Thankfully, Rosewood wasn't far from the pack. It was a nice day, and Peregrine enjoyed the sounds of the forest. Usually he hid in big cities so it would be harder for the people to catch him. There were more people, and he could vanish in the crowd much more easily than he ever could here in Rosewood.

He was nervous when he reached the town. He almost expected someone to jump him and drag him toward a van or car, but nothing happened. He looked up and down Main Street. There wasn't much else in Rosewood, and it was very different from what he was used to, but not in a bad way. People walked around, waving at each other and stopping to chat. It was obvious even from what little Peregrine was seeing now that this was a town where everyone knew everyone and they would notice him. It was tempting to go back to the pack and hide in the forest, but instead, he sucked in a breath, squared his shoulders, and walked down the sidewalk.

There was a park on the other side of the street. It was book-ended by two stores, one a bookstore, the other selling clothes. There were a coffee shop and other shops where Peregrine stood, and he yearned to explore. He didn't have much money, and he never purchased more than he could carry while he was on the run, so he ignored them and headed toward the coffee shop. No matter how nice Cam and Toby were, their coffee couldn't stand up to one professionally made.

Peregrine stepped in, briefly closing his eyes and inhaling the scent of coffee. He realized the mistake he'd made when he opened his eyes again and saw three men staring at him from the table.

Sage, Sam, and Basil.

Peregrine looked away, wondering if he could sneak out before they did anything, but it was too late. They'd seen him, and Basil was already on his feet, coming toward him. "I've never seen you here," he said as a hello.

Peregrine forced himself to smile. "That's because it's the first time I've been here."

"Do Cam and Toby know you're here?"

Peregrine bristled. "They're not my parents. I live with them because I don't have another place to stay, but I don't owe them an explanation or anything else."

Basil raised his hands. "That's not what I meant. They just worry about the people who are after you."

Peregrine sucked in a breath. He shouldn't have snapped the way he had. He'd saved Basil's life recently, and maybe for that, maybe for another reason, Basil had decided the two of them should be friends. He'd been trying to get Peregrine to come out of his shell since he'd arrived in Rosewood, but so far, Peregrine had pushed him away every time. He didn't want to have friends.

Yet, at the same time, he did.

His life was lonely. He never allowed himself to get close to anyone in case he had to run, but he was twenty-nine, and he had no relationships. He didn't have a family. He didn't have friends, let alone a boyfriend.

He was tired.

"Why don't you come to sit with us? We'll grab you a coffee." The corner of Basil's lips curled. "Jarvis makes the best coffee in town."

Peregrine had no idea who Jarvis was, but he found himself nodding before he could think better of it.

Jarvis had noticed Peregrine as soon as he'd walked into the coffee shop. How could he not have? Peregrine was the most beautiful man Jarvis had ever seen. His white-blond hair fell in front of his eyes, and it made Jarvis want to push it away to get Peregrine to look at him. And when he did, he knew he would be confronted with light blue eyes.

But it wasn't just the way Peregrine looked. Jarvis didn't know anything about Peregrine's past, but looking at him was enough to make him realize it hadn't been an easy one. There was a wariness in Peregrine's gaze as he looked around, almost as if trying to find a safe exit, or maybe a threat. Jarvis wouldn't be surprised if that was what Peregrine was doing while Basil dragged him toward the table where he was sitting with Sam and Sage.

Since the day he'd arrived in Rosewood, Peregrine had enthralled Jarvis, but Jarvis had kept his distance. Not only did he know Peregrine probably wouldn't be happy about having someone approach him out of the blue, but he also knew better than to fool himself into thinking Peregrine would give him a second glance.

"Jarvis?"

Jarvis jerked so hard that some of the milk he'd been

pouring into a mug splashed out. He swore and put both the mug and milk down, then looked at Sam.

"Sorry about that," Sam said.

Jarvis shook his head. "It wasn't your fault. Did you need anything?"

Sam gestured toward the table where he and the others were sitting. Peregrine was there now, too, looking uncomfortable and out of place. "Do you think you could make a coffee for Peregrine?"

"Of course. Just give me a second to clean this up."

"We're not going anywhere." Sam paused. "You know, you could sit with us."

Jarvis's heart was in his throat. "I have work to do," he murmured.

Sam looked disappointed. "Maybe next time? We often come during the afternoon, too."

Jarvis nodded, but he still didn't look up. He didn't know why Sam was offering, but he doubted there was anything more than pity behind it. Sam and the others had no doubt noticed that Jarvis didn't spend a lot of time with other people, and they were being nice about it. Jarvis supposed it was better than hearing himself being called a loner or so dull that he didn't have friends, but he still didn't like it.

Jarvis knew he was boring. His siblings had told him every day of his life, and he hadn't needed them to know that. He had eyes, just like everyone else.

But he didn't like self-pity. His life might not be perfect, but he still enjoyed it, and he didn't want it to change.

He quickly got a coffee together for Peregrine. He tried to make it as good as he could. He wanted Peregrine to like it and maybe to think he was good at his job. He didn't dare look at Peregrine when Sam grabbed the coffee and headed back to the table, though. He wanted to, but instead, he finished cleaning the counter, looked around quickly to make sure no one was waiting for coffee, and rushed into the back room.

The door closed behind him, and he sucked in a breath. He had to lean against it because his knees felt like jelly, but thankfully, that passed quickly.

What had Sam been thinking? Jarvis had heard him tell Peregrine that he made the best coffee in town, but that couldn't be right. Jarvis wouldn't say he sucked at his job, but it was just making coffee. There was nothing much to it.

But Peregrine had wanted coffee anyway. Jarvis wondered if he liked it. Maybe he should have stayed to watch and make sure everything was okay. If Peregrine didn't enjoy it, Jarvis could have made something else for him.

But it was too late. Now Jarvis was hiding in the back room, and Peregrine was making friends with the others. It wasn't surprising that was who he gravitated to. Everyone knew Peregrine had saved Basil's life, and Basil and the others were special. They weren't normal wolf shifters like Jarvis. Basil was a rare hybrid, and Sage and Sam were just as rare. It almost felt like everyone in the pack was a special kind of shifter except for Jarvis.

That wasn't the truth, of course. Jarvis was allowing his self-pity to take over, and he had to stop.

He took a deep breath, reached for his hair but gave up when he felt how much of a mess it was, and opened the door. He did his best not to be seen as he took his place behind the counter again, but he failed. He took the risk of looking at the table where Sam and his friends were sitting, and when he did, his gaze crossed with Peregrine's.

Jarvis was frozen. He couldn't have looked away even if he wanted to, and he didn't. He had no idea why. Peregrine was staring at him, but he found he couldn't *not* stare back.

Peregrine leaned closer to Sam without looking away from Jarvis. He asked something, and Sam turned his attention to

Jarvis, too.

That was enough for Jarvis to look away. He had no idea what the two were saying, and he didn't want to find out.

He looked around the coffee shop to make sure no one needed more coffee, but the morning rush was almost over, and the customers still in the shop were sitting at the tables and taking their time. Jarvis might as well start cleaning, so that was what he did. He did his best not to look at the table where the Rosewood pack members were sitting.

They kept peeking at him. He didn't understand why Peregrine would be curious about him. He was making friends with the pack's extraordinary members, and Jarvis knew for sure he wouldn't want to talk to *him*. Maybe he just wanted to thank him for the coffee. It was just making coffee, but Jarvis was good at it.

"Are we making you uncomfortable?"

Jarvis jerked for the second time in a handful of minutes. He peered at Sam, who looked bashful.

"Sorry. I didn't mean to startle you a second time," he said. "I just wanted to know if we're making you uncomfortable, because if that's the case, we can leave."

Jarvis swallowed, but his mouth was dry. He peeked toward the table again, surprised to see that Peregrine was still staring. He looked away, but his heart was racing. "You don't have to go. You're not making me uncomfortable."

"Are you sure? Because you look flustered."

"I'm fine," Jarvis snapped. He took a deep breath and looked Sam in the eyes. "I swear I am. I would never ask customers to go."

Sam looked at him for a moment, then slowly nodded. "All right. We're about to go anyway. I have my healing lesson this morning."

Sam was studying with his brother to become a healer, so they spent a lot of time pouring over books and helping the

Rosewood pack healer. Jarvis had never needed them, and he hoped he never would. "I'll see you soon," he said.

Sam smiled. "Probably. And thank you for the coffee. It was delicious, like always."

Jarvis felt his cheeks heat, and he looked away. By the time he peered at Sam again, Sam had stepped back to the table and was talking with his friends. Sage and Basil got up. They were still talking to Peregrine, but to Jarvis's surprise, he didn't go with them. Instead, he stayed in his seat as they headed toward the door, alone.

What did that mean?

Peregrine didn't want to go back to pack territory just yet, which was why he stayed in the coffee shop when the others left. As soon as the door was closed behind them, he took a deep breath and relaxed. He took a sip of coffee — which really was as good as Sam and the others had promised — and looked around.

He'd noticed Jarvis, and he didn't know what to make of the man. Jarvis kept peeking at the table as if he wanted to come over to talk to them, but he hadn't. Instead, he'd disappeared in the backroom for a while, and when Sam had gone to ask him if they were making him uncomfortable, he'd said they weren't. Peregrine was pretty sure that was a lie, but he wasn't about to push. He wasn't Jarvis's friend, and he probably never would be.

Jarvis was great at making coffee, though.

Peregrine finished his coffee. He could feel Jarvis's gaze on him, but he was used to being stared at, and he wasn't offended. Sam had explained that Jarvis was a pack member, so he had to know who Peregrine was and probably what he could do. He was no doubt curious, which was always the case when Peregrine met new people.

But Peregrine had finished his coffee, and he wanted more. He looked around. The coffee shop wasn't empty, but all the customers were sitting at tables, either reading books or working on their computers. The counter was empty except for Jarvis, and Peregrine was almost a hundred percent sure Jarvis wouldn't do anything to hurt him. It would probably be a miracle if Jarvis managed to talk to him. From what Peregrine had seen, Jarvis was shy.

Peregrine liked that. There was nothing he hated more than men who thought they were a gift to humanity. Usually, they were the worst people. Jarvis didn't look like he was like that, and Peregrine didn't miss the way he kept peeking over as he got to his feet and moved toward the counter. Jarvis tensed more with every step Peregrine took until he looked like he might break if Peregrine as much as touched him.

Peregrine didn't know what to think about it, but he was amused. Most people would have come straight up to Peregrine and asked him questions, but Jarvis hadn't. Instead, he kept his distance, allowing Peregrine to go to him instead of the other way around. It was a nice change, and it made Peregrine curious.

He knew he couldn't afford to make friends, but talking to Jarvis wasn't making friends with him.

"Hello," he said when he reached the counter.

Jarvis had to look at him this time. When he did, Peregrine was delighted to see his cheeks were pink. It was adorable — not that Jarvis needed to blush to be adorable.

Some people might call Jarvis plain, but Peregrine wouldn't. He liked Jarvis's brown hair and eyes. He liked that Jarvis was taller than him, but not as thin. He especially liked the way Jarvis kept staring at him as if he was something special. Peregrine was nothing to write home about. Jarvis didn't seem to think so, and it was a pleasant feeling.

"Hello," Jarvis croaked.

Peregrine kept smiling. "I'm Peregrine. I'm living with the pack at the moment," he murmured.

Jarvis nodded. "I know. I'm a pack member." He paused. "Welcome."

It sounded more like a question than a welcome, but Peregrine smiled anyway. "Thank you. I'd like another coffee if it's possible."

"Of course."

Jarvis went to work immediately, and Peregrine saw him relax as he moved. He was in his element behind the counter, and watching him as he got the coffee ready was enjoyable.

Once he was done, he put the coffee Peregrine had ordered on the counter, then added a brownie. Peregrine looked from the brownie to Jarvis's face. Jarvis wasn't looking at him anymore, but he didn't need to.

"I didn't order the brownie," Peregrine said.

Jarvis shrugged. "You don't have to eat it if you don't want it, but I thought it would be nice."

"You're right. It *is* nice, and I didn't expect it. Thank you."

Jarvis nodded. He didn't add anything, but that didn't change the fact that Peregrine thought he was cute and quiet, which was the kind of guy he preferred. As overwhelming as Basil and his friends were, Jarvis was the opposite, and being with him made Peregrine relax.

Peregrine bit his lower lip. He wanted to ask Jarvis to be his friend. It wasn't the best idea, but Peregrine wanted someone who could help him get used to living in Rosewood, maybe someone who could explain who was who in the pack, things like that. Toby and Cam would help if he asked, but they were both busy, and Peregrine didn't want to ask too much of them. He could ask Basil and the others, but he *wanted* to ask Jarvis.

There wasn't a reason for him to, and he should probably step back and leave Jarvis alone, but he wanted to try.

Peregrine hadn't allowed himself to have anything he wanted in a long time, and while he knew it was a bad idea to do this with Jarvis, he couldn't stop himself from asking, "Do you have a minute?"

Jarvis looked at Peregrine again. His brown eyes were soft and gentle. "Did you need anything?"

"I wanted to talk to you."

Jarvis gaped for a second before schooling his expression. "Of course. You can talk to me, but I'm sure Sam and the others would be better. They know everyone in the pack, and they're more important."

Peregrine frowned. "What do you mean?"

Jarvis shrugged. "You don't have to be nice. I know I'm just a wolf shifter, and I make coffee for a living. I'm not like Sam and Toby, who can heal people. I'm not like Basil, who's, well, special. I'm just me."

And Peregrine quite enjoyed it. He suspected saying that to Jarvis would send him running, though, so he kept it to himself. "That's why I can't ask them. They're also very busy, and I don't want to impose."

Jarvis's eyebrows rose on his forehead. "But you won't mind imposing on me?" His eyes widened. "Not that you would. I don't have anything to do. Well, anything apart from making coffee. It's not a problem. You can ask me whatever you need."

Peregrine pressed his lips together. He didn't want to laugh or even smile. He didn't want Jarvis to think he was making fun of him. He just really enjoyed talking to Jarvis. "So you know I'm new in town. I don't want to take time away from Sam and Toby, considering what they're studying, and while I'm sure Basil would show me around, he's as new as me."

Jarvis stared. "You want someone to show you around?"

"Yes, but I don't want to take too much of your time."

"You wouldn't. It's just that there's not much to see. Rosewood is kind of tiny, and since you're on Main Street, you've already seen everything there is to see."

Jarvis was making it hard for Peregrine to spend time with him. Peregrine didn't think it was on purpose, which made him want to do it even more. "That's fine. I just want to know where everything is." And where he could escape if he needed to.

The thought was enough to make Peregrine sober up. He liked Jarvis, and seeing how flustered Jarvis was made Peregrine want to kiss him, but he couldn't afford to do that. It would hurt too much if he had to leave, and he always did.

So there couldn't be anything between him and Jarvis, but that didn't mean they couldn't be friendly. Jarvis looked like he needed one, and Peregrine knew *he* did.

"I can do that," Jarvis said slowly. "But not right now. I have to finish my shift."

"That's fine. I'll grab my coffee and brownie and sit back down. I can wait for you there."

Jarvis blinked. "You're not going back to the pack?"

"Not unless you want me to."

Jarvis hesitated, then shook his head. "You can stay at the table. I'll come to you as soon as I'm done."

Peregrine was relieved. No matter how bad an idea this was, he wanted it to happen. He wanted to spend time with Jarvis and be a normal person for once in his life.

It wouldn't last long, but at least he would know what he was missing once he had to flee.

Jarvis didn't know what to think of Peregrine's request. It didn't make sense. Even if Peregrine was a bother, he was friends with Sam and the others. Jarvis was sure they would find a way to show him around without taking time away from their jobs and studies.

And even if they couldn't, why was Peregrine asking him of all people to show him around town and pack territory? Anyone would have been better. Even Jarvis's siblings would have been better. He didn't know how old Peregrine was, but he had to be older than Jarvis, maybe around the age of Jarvis's brother Todd. It would make more sense for them to spend time together than it would for Jarvis and Peregrine.

But Peregrine had asked so gently and nicely that Jarvis couldn't say no. He had no idea what would happen, but he would find out soon enough. It wasn't like Peregrine had asked him to become his best friend, anyway. He just needed help to find his bearings, and once that was done, Jarvis doubted they would ever talk again.

His shift had never felt so long. He kept watching the clock, then peeking at Peregrine, wondering if he was bored. He didn't seem to be. He'd grabbed one of the books the coffee shop owner kept on the shelves against the walls, and he was reading. He looked up a few times and noticed Jarvis was staring at him, but he limited himself to smiling and going back to the book.

Jarvis still didn't know what to think by the time his shift was over, but he was relieved anyway. He went to the backroom to put down his apron and grab his backpack, but he got Peregrine another coffee before going back to him. Even if he wasn't finished drinking the last one he'd gotten, it was cold by now.

Jarvis walked over to Peregrine, still watching him. Peregrine was so engrossed in his book that he didn't realize Jarvis was there until Jarvis stood right next to him.

"I'm done," Jarvis said.

Peregrine jerked. His elbow knocked against Jarvis's arm, and Jarvis dropped the coffee. He scrambled back as it splashed all over the floor. He and Peregrine stared at it, then they moved at the same time, both of them reaching down to clean up. Jarvis didn't have the time to move back when he realized what was about to happen, and his forehead hit Peregrine's. At the same time, he smelled the one thing he'd never thought he'd smell — his mate. He couldn't think about that right now, and he wasn't ready to believe the scent came from the man in front of him. It just wasn't possible.

Jarvis jerked back, holding a hand to his head. It hurt, but he didn't care. He wanted to make sure he hadn't hurt Peregrine.

"I'm sorry," he said. He should have known he would cause a disaster. He always did. "Are you hurt? Do you need ice?"

To Jarvis's surprise, Peregrine started laughing. "I'm fine," he said between two snickers. "We're disasters, though, aren't we?"

Jarvis found himself smiling. Maybe he'd been wrong and Peregrine wasn't his mate. Peregrine hadn't said anything, and he'd have smelled, Jarvis since Jarvis had smelled him. "I don't know about you, but this is pretty normal for me." He looked at the floor. "I'm going to grab the mop and clean this up. We can go right after I'm done, or maybe you want to go home? I wouldn't blame you since I just head-butted you."

Peregrine shook his head. "I'm not going anywhere, and I'll help you clean up."

Jarvis stared. He'd expected Peregrine to have had enough of him already, but instead, he was still smiling. What the fuck was going on? This wasn't Jarvis's life. He didn't have friends, and he didn't make people laugh, except when he fell on his face.

"You don't have to help me," Jarvis said.

"I don't mind. It was my fault, after all."

"I shouldn't have startled you."

"It's fine," Peregrine said. "You grab the mop. I'll throw

away the cup and use napkins to get a start."

Jarvis couldn't leave a mess, so he headed back to the backroom. By the time he was back with Peregrine, most of the coffee wasn't on the floor anymore. Peregrine had dragged one of the trash cans closer, and he'd dumped all the wet napkins he'd used and the now-empty cup into it. He smiled when he heard Jarvis come closer, and Jarvis couldn't help but ask, "Why me?" Because if they weren't mates, it didn't make sense.

Peregrine frowned. "I'm not sure what you're asking."

"I know you said you didn't want to be a bother to the others, but I'm sure they wouldn't mind. And even if they did, why did you ask me to show you around? I'm sure pretty much anyone else in the pack would have been better."

Peregrine stared at Jarvis, so much so that Jarvis started cleaning the floor just to do something. He could feel Peregrine's gaze on his face, and it was heavy and incomprehensible.

"I don't know about you, but I don't have friends," Peregrine finally said.

Jarvis barked out a laugh. "If you want to know how to make friends, I'm the wrong person to ask. I don't have friends, either."

Peregrine frowned. "I don't understand why. You're a nice person."

"You don't know me. But you've seen what a disaster I am already. It makes sense that no one wants to spend time with me."

Peregrine shook his head. "It doesn't. You dropped a coffee. No one died, and nothing bad happened. I don't understand why you're so negative about yourself, but I suppose I'll find out once we're friends."

Jarvis didn't want Peregrine to find out anything. He doubted Peregrine would want to spend any amount of time with him once he did, but he couldn't find it in himself to say that he didn't want to see Peregrine again. It would be a lie. He wanted to spend time with Peregrine and get to know him.

It wasn't just because Peregrine was a rare shifter, because he was a healer, or even because he was gorgeous. There was something about him—something gentle and nice—that attracted Jarvis more than everything else put together. He still didn't understand how Peregrine thought or why he'd asked him of all people to be friends, but until Peregrine decided otherwise, Jarvis wasn't going anywhere.

Maybe they *were* mates after all. Gosh, this was so confusing.

"Unless you'd rather not be friends with me?" Peregrine asked. There was pain in his voice, but also resignation. "I'd understand. I realize I'm weird, and being friends with me is probably dangerous. Some people would do a lot to get their hands on me because of what I can do. It would be safer for you to stay away from me."

Was that why Peregrine didn't have friends? Because no one wanted to be close to him when people might try to kidnap him? Jarvis found himself angry at the thought. People should be grateful for Peregrine's presence in their life. It didn't have anything to do with him being a healer, but everything with him being a good person. It would be easy for Peregrine to decide he never wanted to heal anyone again so he could stay out of trouble. Instead, he'd helped Basil, and he'd almost been captured because of it.

"I want to be your friend," Jarvis said, sounding more convinced than he was. This was what Peregrine needed, and Jarvis wanted to give it to him.

"Are you sure?" Peregrine sounded hesitant. "Because I *would* understand if it were better for you to stay away from me. You don't have to say yes to being my friend just because I asked."

Jarvis put the mop back into the bucket and looked right at Peregrine, something he'd avoided doing until now. "I don't want to be your friend just because you asked. I've wanted to get to know you since you arrived in Rosewood, so this is perfect."

"Why do you want to get to know me?"

Jarvis shrugged. He didn't know how to answer that without sounding like a creep. "Why do *you* want to get to know me?"

Peregrine stared for a moment. Then, he smiled. "I suppose you're right. Friends, then?"

Jarvis couldn't believe this, but he found himself nodding anyway. "Friends," he confirmed.

"For now," Peregrine added.

Jarvis licked his lips. "What does that mean?"

Peregrine's lips curled. "We'll have to talk about the fact that we're mates eventually, but for now, this is fine."

Jarvis swallowed. He wasn't wrong after all.

Chapter Two

Peregrine wouldn't say he felt at home, but having spent a few weeks with the pack meant he was more comfortable with them. He was so comfortable that when he'd been invited to a cook-out at the fire pit, he hadn't even freaked out at the thought of being surrounded by a crowd of people he didn't know. He wasn't *entirely* comfortable, but he was getting there, which surprised and worried him.

He shouldn't be feeling at home. He couldn't afford to, not when he might have to run away. He didn't know when, but he'd never been able to stay in one place for long, and he doubted this time would be different. Sure, as long as he didn't heal anyone, he was safe, but what were the odds that no one in the pack would get ill? It always happened, and Peregrine could never say no. How could he? He had the ability to heal people, even from illnesses that should be fatal. He was one of the few who could do it, and while he didn't understand how it worked, he couldn't change what he was or what he could do.

But no matter how comfortable he was starting to feel, he still felt better only with a few people around, especially Jarvis.

He knew Jarvis didn't understand why Peregrine insisted on spending so much time with him, and, to be honest, he wasn't sure himself. There was the mate bond, but both of them had carefully avoided mentioning anything about that since that day at the coffee shop.

But Peregrine had never been closer to anyone than he was

to Jarvis. They hadn't known each other long enough to be really close, but Peregrine couldn't deny he felt safe when he was with Jarvis. It was the mate bond at play, and he didn't know what to think about it.

Jarvis would never ask him to heal anyone. Hell, he probably wouldn't ask Peregrine to heal *him* if he was sick. Peregrine was going to miss Jarvis when he left—because he would eventually, which was why he tried to ignore the mate bond. It was best for both of them to act as if it didn't exist.

Jarvis was adorable and gentle, but he was always down on himself and had no self-esteem. It made Peregrine want to protect him, and he'd never felt that way for anyone. Instead of being the one who needed protection, he was the one offering it, for once. Not that he'd ever say that to Jarvis. Jarvis already thought so little of himself that Peregrine wouldn't want to risk it.

Peregrine didn't understand why Jarvis thought and behaved the way he did. As far as he'd seen, everyone in the pack was friendly. At the very least, they'd been nice to him. He and Jarvis had been spending time together, and from what Peregrine had observed, most people were nice to Jarvis, too. But he didn't know Jarvis's family, so he might be wrong.

The thought of Jarvis's family treating him badly made Peregrine want to find out about them. He looked away from his coffee and toward Jarvis, who was working the morning shift. They were meeting for lunch, and once they were done eating, they would head back to pack territory together.

Peregrine enjoyed spending time at the coffee shop almost as much as he enjoyed spending time with Jarvis. Often, the two meant the same thing. He loved watching Jarvis work because, during those moments, Jarvis stopped being so self-conscious. He focused on the job, and Peregrine could see him visibly relax as he did so.

Then, usually, Jarvis noticed Peregrine watching him and

tensed again.

Peregrine sighed and took another sip of coffee. He kept peeking at Jarvis, who knew he was there but wasn't giving him attention, which was how Peregrine wanted things. His presence was usually distracting, and as much as he enjoyed seeing Jarvis flustered by him, he didn't want him to be in trouble because he couldn't focus.

"You're staring," Sage said.

Sage was already at the coffee shop when Peregrine had arrived, and he hadn't been able to avoid sitting with him, especially since both of them were alone. He didn't know why Sage was here without his friends, and he wasn't about to ask.

Sage was friendly, just like everyone else, and if Peregrine had any intention of staying, he thought he and Sage could become friends. He didn't want to risk it, though. He was already taking too much of a risk getting to know Jarvis. It would break him to lose two people important to him.

One was going to be bad enough.

"We're friends," he said, hoping it would be a good enough explanation. He wasn't about to tell anyone he and Jarvis were mates.

Sage smiled. He blew on the steam rising from his herbal tea before answering. "I don't think I stare at my friends the way you stare at him."

Peregrine wasn't offended. He was new to the pack, while Jarvis had been born in it. Everyone knew him, and it was normal for some of them to be protective. It made the way Jarvis behaved and thought even stranger, and Peregrine wondered if Sage knew something about it. "Can you tell me about Jarvis's family?"

Sage blinked, clearly surprised at the way the conversation was going. "Shouldn't you be asking *him* that?"

"If I do, he's just going to say how marvelous they are and how different he is from them. I want someone to be objective about it."

Sage grimaced. "I don't know if I can be. I don't hate them, exactly, but they're not my favorite people. Besides, while I've been here longer than you, I wasn't born here. They're not part of my friends' group, and I don't know them that well."

"Just tell me what you do know."

Sage nodded and took a sip of tea. Peregrine wrinkled his nose, because that thing stank, but he wasn't one drinking it, thankfully.

"Well, Jarvis still has both his parents and siblings. One sister and two brothers, to be precise. His sister is married and has a child herself, but as far as I know, the brothers are still single." He paused and looked at Peregrine. "Unless Jarvis isn't?"

Peregrine shook his head. "We're just friends."

Sage slowly nodded. "You know no one would care if you and Jarvis were together, right? There are plenty of same-sex couples in the pack."

Peregrine was touched that Sage thought he didn't want to out Jarvis, but there really wasn't anything between them. There couldn't be. "Tell me about Jarvis's brothers," he said instead of answering. They were the most obvious when it came to dealing with Jarvis's self-esteem. Peregrine didn't have brothers, but didn't they tease each other and things like that?

Sage didn't look surprised this time. "There's not much I can tell you. Jarvis is the second youngest. Todd is older by a few years, while Kyle is younger by more or less the same. I don't know how close they are, but I can't say I've ever seen them together."

Peregrine nodded. He noticed Jarvis taking off his apron and smiled, straightening in his chair. That could only mean one thing—Jarvis's shift was over, and they were about to get lunch.

Sage chuckled. "You should go to him."

"What about you?"

"I'll head home soon. Reece doesn't like me spending a lot of time away from him and Carey."

Peregrine knew Sage had two boyfriends—or did he call them mates? And he couldn't imagine how that worked. It felt like a lot of work to have one, let alone two, especially when one was a phoenix shifter. He could tell Sage was happy, though, and he wasn't about to ask questions he shouldn't be asking, no matter how curious he was.

"It was nice talking to you," he said as he got to his feet.

"I hope we can do it again." Sage hesitated. "I know you don't think you'll be staying for long, but even if you don't, it doesn't mean you can't have friends."

"Thank you," Peregrine answered. What else could he say? Everyone had been friendly and had tried getting closer to him, but he couldn't allow it. It was already a big risk for him to be friends with Jarvis, and he couldn't afford to open up even more. It would be bad enough to lose Jarvis.

Peregrine had never had a friend, and he'd never had a best friend like Jarvis was now. He knew that if he allowed things to continue, there would be more than friendship between them, especially with the bond at play.

It was too dangerous, and it would hurt too much.

Jarvis had noticed Peregrine talking with Sage, and he wondered what they'd been saying. He doubted it had anything to do with him. He wasn't that interesting, and he didn't know Sage well. Peregrine had looked relaxed, though, and Jarvis couldn't help but wonder if he was when they were together, too.

Usually, he seemed to be. Jarvis didn't understand it, and he wasn't sure he wanted to. He and Peregrine were friends—

nothing more—but he knew it was only for as long as Peregrine was in town. He didn't fool himself into thinking Peregrine wasn't going to run eventually, no matter what was between them. Even though they'd known each other for only a few weeks, they'd been spending a lot of time together, and Jarvis was starting to understand Peregrine.

He wanted to help. Even after explaining that using his healing magic was how the people after him found him, Jarvis had still admitted he would heal anyone who needed it. Jarvis was in awe. He didn't think he'd survive if he was on the run for most of his life, yet Peregrine had, and he was ready to sacrifice his freedom and happiness to help people. He was a better man than Jarvis could ever be, and it made Jarvis fall in love with him just a bit more. It had nothing to do with the bond and everything to do with the kind of person Peregrine was.

Jarvis had never been in love. He wasn't sure that was what he felt when it came to Peregrine, but it might as well be. He wanted to spend all his time with Peregrine. He wanted to make him smile, laugh, and make him happy. Surely, that meant he was in love?

But he couldn't say anything about that or their bond. He didn't want to lose Peregrine's friendship, and he didn't want to make him run. Peregrine seemed to have finally found a home with the pack, at least temporarily, and Jarvis didn't want to do anything to make him uncomfortable or scared.

"I thought you were done," Peregrine said from behind Jarvis, making him jump.

Thankfully, Jarvis wasn't holding anything but his apron this time, so it wasn't a disaster when it fell to the floor. Jarvis still felt his cheeks heat, but he kept his gaze away from Peregrine as he leaned down and picked it up.

"I'll just put this in the backroom," he said.

When he finally turned to Peregrine, Peregrine was

smiling. "I'll be here."

Jarvis nodded and rushed into the back room. Amanda, who worked the next shift, was there, pulling her apron on. She turned when she heard him and smiled, but it was nothing like Peregrine's smile. "How was the morning?" she asked.

"Busy enough that we should talk to Diego about hiring more people."

Amanda grimaced. "You know he won't."

"I do." Their boss was notorious for hiring as few people as possible and paying those who worked for him the minimum acceptable. Jarvis wished he could quit this job, but he enjoyed it, and there wasn't much else he could find in Rosewood.

"I just hope those guys won't come in again," Amanda said.

Jarvis frowned. "What guys?"

"I don't know. They came in the other afternoon, looking around and asking a lot of questions. They wanted to know about new people in town, and I pointed out *they* were new. They weren't happy. I haven't seen them again, but they creeped me out."

Jarvis bit his lower lip. It probably was nothing, but he couldn't help but worry about Peregrine.

He pushed that worry to the back of his mind. He and Peregrine were having lunch together before going back to pack territory. Peregrine no doubt had more important and interesting things to do this afternoon, but Jarvis was grateful they were spending time together. He didn't know how much longer Peregrine would stay, and he wanted to take advantage of every second he could.

He and Amanda went back to the front at the same time. Jarvis walked around the counter and joined Peregrine, who was leaning against it. He looked up and smiled when he heard Jarvis — taking Jarvis's breath away.

He was beautiful. Jarvis didn't think he'd ever seen anyone so gorgeous, even though there were plenty of pretty guys in the pack. Peregrine was different, although probably only to Jarvis.

"Ready to go?" Peregrine asked.

"Ready. What do you have in mind for lunch?"

Peregrine's smile widened. "I found a Chinese restaurant close by."

"I like Chinese." And Jarvis thought he knew which restaurant Peregrine was talking about. It wasn't like there were dozens of them in town, and if there had been, Jarvis would have eaten at all of them. He enjoyed trying different places and foods, which was why he was overweight.

Peregrine didn't say anything about that, though. Instead, he left the coffee shop, and Jarvis followed him.

"I have a question for you," Peregrine asked.

"I'm listening." Jarvis would answer any question Peregrine had if he could.

"Why do you talk about yourself the way you do?"

That wasn't a question Jarvis had expected. "What do you mean?"

"You talk about yourself as if you don't matter. You put yourself down, and I don't understand why."

Jarvis shrugged. "I'm not special like you or Sage and Sam and the others. I'm not funny like my brother. I'm not pretty like my sister. I'm just me, and I'm nothing special."

Jarvis was surprised when Peregrine's expression shifted to anger. He briefly wondered if Peregrine was angry at *him*, and he was relieved when Peregrine huffed and smoothed out his expression.

"Who told you all those things?" Peregrine asked.

"No one. They don't need to tell me because I have eyes. I can see how bland I am. It's not a problem, though. It means people don't usually see me, but that's mostly fine with me." Except for Peregrine. He saw Jarvis much more than many people, including Jarvis's family.

"You're the best person I know," Peregrine said, his voice strong as if he was convinced of what he was saying. "You're nice and kind. That's really all that matters when it comes to people, I think."

Jarvis found himself smiling. "Thank you." He wished Peregrine also found him handsome, but he wasn't an idiot. He *wasn't* handsome. He was boring through and through, and that included the way he looked. He had brown eyes, like just about everyone else in the world. He had brown hair, and no matter how much he tried to style it, it never looked decent. And of course, there was the rest of his body. He didn't hate it, but he knew he wasn't anything to call home about.

Jarvis understood why Peregrine hadn't mentioned their bond again. He was happy just being friends with Peregrine. He didn't need anything else, although it would hurt when Peregrine eventually found someone. Jarvis was already in love with him. He doubted that would change as long as they spent time together, and maybe even if they stopped. Peregrine was special, and just like he'd told Jarvis, he was nice and kind. It was all Jarvis had ever wanted in a person, and Peregrine was the perfect boyfriend.

But not for Jarvis.

"I saw you and Sage were talking," he said, trying to change the topic of the conversation.

Peregrine watched him as they walked down the sidewalk, and Jarvis wondered if he was going to push. Thankfully, he didn't. Instead, he sighed. "I couldn't avoid him, not when he was sitting alone when I walked into the coffee shop."

Jarvis frowned. "I thought the two of you were friends."

"We're friendly. I really have only one friend, and it's you."

Being friends with your mate had to be as good as actually

being with him, right? "Sage is a good person." He was sweet, and he'd never been mean to Jarvis.

"I'm sure he is, and he's trying hard to make me feel welcome. I'm just not used to having friends, you know? It's strange to spend time talking with people, and I'm never sure what to do or say."

"You don't seem to have a problem with that when you're with me."

Peregrine smiled. "That's because you're special."

For one moment, Jarvis believed him.

Peregrine didn't mind talking about himself, but he wanted to talk about Jarvis more. Jarvis was still smiling after Peregrine told him he was special, and Peregrine wanted him to continue feeling that way. He wasn't ready to talk about their bond yet, but he would be soon. He knew he could trust Jarvis now. It didn't help with everything else, but it wouldn't be fair to Jarvis to continue behaving as if they weren't mates. "Tell me more about you," he said.

That just about swept the smile off Jarvis's face. "You already know everything there is to know about me."

"I don't think that's true. We never talked about your family, for example." Peregrine felt a bit guilty because he suspected Jarvis's family was the reason he had such low self-esteem, but the thought made him angry.

Families should be loving. They should be there for each other and push each other up, but instead, it felt like Jarvis's didn't even like him, let alone want him to be happy. Peregrine could be wrong, and he wanted to hear what Jarvis thought of his parents and siblings.

Jarvis grimaced. "I don't want to talk about them. Maybe we could talk about *your* family."

Peregrine stared at him for a moment. "There's nothing to

say."

"I'm sure that's not true."

Peregrine shook his head. "I mean that. I've never met either of my parents, and I don't know if I have siblings. When I was a kid, I belonged to a guy. He was old and sick, and he forced me to heal him again and again."

"That's horrible." Jarvis looked like he was about to cry.

Peregrine acted instinctively, taking one of Jarvis's hands as they continued walking. This wasn't the best place to have this conversation, and Peregrine had never told anyone about his life, but he trusted Jarvis.

The thought stunned him. He'd never trusted anyone. He'd barely even trusted Basil and the others, but he'd healed Basil, and they'd promised to help him. They had, at least for now.

But Jarvis was different, and Peregrine found himself spilling out his entire history. "It was. I was with him until I turned seven. Then even I couldn't do anything for him, and he died. His daughter didn't know what to do with me, but one of his business partners offered to take me on. I stayed with that guy until I was fourteen. He made people pay him for me to heal them."

"We don't have to talk about it if you don't want to," Jarvis said. His voice was heavy, and when Peregrine looked at him, his eyes glittered with tears.

Peregrine looked around. They'd been headed toward the restaurant, but instead of continuing, he pulled Jarvis toward the park. They'd been exploring it every time they spent time together, which was almost every day. Peregrine knew where to go, and they walked until he found the bench hidden in the middle of the trees. It was stone, so it was hard, but Peregrine didn't mind. He sat, pulling Jarvis along. Jarvis wasn't looking at him, so Peregrine leaned down until he could look Jarvis in the eyes.

They were still full of tears, which made Peregrine feel horrible. "I'm not telling you this to make you cry or to make you feel sorry for me," he explained.

Jarvis shook his head and rubbed his eyes. "I'm sorry. I know it's ridiculous. It didn't happen to me, and I shouldn't be crying."

Peregrine didn't think that. He thought Jarvis was a kind person, and he was touched he felt so strongly about something that was in the past. "I escaped at fourteen." Jarvis looked at him, and now that Peregrine had his attention, he continued his story. "An old man couldn't be moved, so they had to take me to him. When I took his illness away, I flew through the house until I found an open window. It was summer, so it was easy. I left through the window, and I never went back."

"But you've been on the run since then."

Peregrine shrugged. "Maybe, but at least I'm free."

"I don't understand how the people after you can find you every time you heal or who they are."

"I'm not sure who they are," Peregrine said slowly. He'd asked himself that question plenty of times, but he still didn't have an answer. He suspected there wasn't one. Many different people wanted what he could do, and all of them tried to get their hands on him. "But I know how to define it. When I take away an illness and dissipate it, it's magic. I don't know how it works, just how to do it. The people after me use witches and mages. They find the magic I emanate after I take the illness, and they follow it."

"So as long as you don't heal anyone, they can't find you."

"Which is why I'm safe here as long as I don't."

"But once you do, you'll have to run."

Peregrine's chest squeezed at the thought. "Exactly. I'm used to it, but I'm not looking forward to it."

"You don't ever have to heal anyone you don't want to

heal."

Peregrine smiled. "But don't you see? I *want* to help people. I want to heal them. I have the ability to do it, and I don't want people to suffer when I can stop it."

Jarvis looked fierce now. "But it's not fair to you. You shouldn't have to be on the run for the rest of your life."

"I hope I won't be." But seeing Jarvis so angry on his behalf made him want so much more than what he had, even now.

It was easy to imagine staying in Rosewood. It was even easier to imagine being with Jarvis, and not just as friends. Even now, they were still holding hands, and Jarvis's touch was strong but gentle. He knew most shifters thought that being mates meant you'd found the one perfect person made for you in the world, and he hadn't believed it. He wasn't sure he did even now, but spending time with Jarvis was making him change his mind.

But Peregrine knew better than to hope he could really stay. He would have to leave eventually, and he didn't want to break Jarvis's heart, or even his own. It might be too late for his, but if he could shield Jarvis from the pain of losing him, he would.

Peregrine's mouth went dry. He could see himself being so happy in Rosewood, and it scared him to allow himself to even think about it.

"Cam knows about this, right?" Jarvis asked.

"He does. He promised he wouldn't ask me to heal anyone."

"See? You're safe with us."

Peregrine knew he was. He also knew that people got ill, and that eventually he would feel the need to use his power. It was a problem he didn't want to think about right now.

He got to his feet. "How about we go eat something? I don't know about you, but I'm starving."

Jarvis got up, too. He rubbed his face with his free hand.

Then he seemed to realize Peregrine still held the other. He snatched his away, his cheeks red, and while Peregrine missed the contact, he enjoyed watching how flustered Jarvis was.

"You're right. We should go eat. I don't want you to be hungry."

Peregrine smiled and shook his head. "How about you? Aren't you hungry?"

Jarvis shrugged and patted his stomach. "Even though I am, it's not like I'm going to starve if I skip lunch."

They started walking again, but Peregrine was frowning. "I don't like you talking about yourself that way," he eventually said.

"What way?" Jarvis asked as they reached the sidewalk.

"Like you just did, saying you're fat in an underhanded way. You're not fat."

"I'm not blind. I see myself in the mirror every day. I know I am, but that's okay."

Peregrine agreed it was. He liked Jarvis's body the way it was, and he didn't want Jarvis to change it if he didn't want to. He also didn't want Jarvis to talk about himself the way he did.

"Has someone been telling you these things?" he asked.

"What things?"

"That you're fat and boring. All those things."

Peregrine twisted to look at Jarvis when he answered. Maybe he'd pushed too much, but they were friends, and he didn't want Jarvis to think so badly of himself. Jarvis was the most gentle person Peregrine knew, but he was only gentle with other people, never with himself.

Peregrine's foot slipped on the edge of the sidewalk. He yelped and reached out, trying to grab Jarvis's hand, but it was too late. He saw the car approaching as he fell, and he closed his eyes.

Jarvis didn't hesitate. He couldn't, not when Peregrine's life was in danger.

He jumped forward, putting himself in front of Peregrine. He managed to grab Peregrine's waist and push him toward the sidewalk just as the car hit him.

His world exploded. His legs went up in flames, or at least, it felt like they did. He fell to the ground, his lower body a ball of pain. He sucked in a breath, then another, trying to breathe through it. At least the car had stopped. Things could be much worse, although he didn't know how bad they were just yet.

"Jarvis?"

Peregrine sounded panicked, and Jarvis opened his eyes to look at him. He hadn't even realized he'd closed them.

Peregrine was kneeling next to him, his hands hovering over Jarvis's chest as if he wasn't sure whether or not he should touch him. Jarvis wanted him to, but he didn't want to ask and make Peregrine uncomfortable.

"Jarvis? Can you hear me?" Peregrine asked.

Jarvis opened his mouth to answer, but only a croak came out. He closed it again, licked his lips, and tried a second time. "I'm fine."

Peregrine didn't look like he believed Jarvis, so Jarvis tried to move into a sitting position. Peregrine pushed him back onto the ground, for which Jarvis was grateful, because it hurt too much for him to sit. He wondered if he'd broken something. Even if he had, it was worth it. This way, Peregrine wasn't the one hurting.

"I called an ambulance," a woman said.

Jarvis rolled his head to try to find her, but he couldn't see her. There were a lot of people around him and Peregrine, and of course, the car that had hit him. An older man stood next to the driver's door, twisting his hands together. When he noticed Jarvis was looking at him, he sucked in a breath. "I'm so sorry. You fell on the road in front of me so quickly that I didn't have the time to stop the car before it hit you."

Jarvis swallowed. "It's fine."

A hand landed on Jarvis's chest, and he looked at Peregrine. His expression was still horrified, but there was strength and conviction in it now. Jarvis didn't know what that meant, so he asked. "What?"

Peregrine looked around. "I'm going to step away and shift."

It took Jarvis a second to understand what Peregrine was saying. "But I'm not ill. You can't do anything for me."

"I can't heal you, but I can take the pain away. It's the least I can do, since I should be the one in your place."

He started to get up, but Jarvis caught his hand and shook his head. It hurt, even though he hadn't been hit on the head. "You can't do that. They'll find you."

He wasn't strong enough to keep Peregrine with him at the moment, and Peregrine gently let go of Jarvis's hand. "I know. This is worth it, though."

Jarvis couldn't say he enjoyed being in pain, but his brain was stuck on what would happen once Peregrine took the pain away.

The people who were after him would find him, and he would have to run. He'd have to leave Rosewood and Jarvis behind, and Jarvis doubted he would ever see him again. He didn't want to lose Peregrine, but he couldn't stop him. The only thing he could do was watch him walk away and turn a corner.

Jarvis closed his eyes and tried to swallow again. It hurt, but he wasn't sure what hurt more—his legs or his heart. He kept his eyes closed until something landed on his chest. He already knew what he would see when he opened his eyes, so he did.

A white bird was sitting on his chest. It was staring at Jarvis in a way only one person looked at him.

Jarvis sighed. "You shouldn't do this," he said.

Peregrine continued staring. Luckily, the people around Jarvis were distracted, talking to each other about what had happened and how horrible it had been. They didn't see Peregrine start glowing. They didn't see Jarvis's body slump in relief when the pain leaked out of him. Peregrine stayed where he was until Jarvis couldn't feel anything, then he flew away, taking to the sky.

Jarvis knew his legs were still broken, but he didn't care. Peregrine had risked everything to help him, and he didn't know if he would be able to repay him for that.

"What happened?" a voice asked.

Jarvis blinked and looked up to see Sam and his mate standing over him. Frederic was already on the phone while Sam knelt next to Jarvis.

"What happened?" Sam asked again.

Jarvis licked his lips. "The car. Peregrine slipped off the sidewalk, but I managed to pull him away from the car."

"And you put yourself into its trajectory instead."

It wasn't a question, but Jarvis nodded anyway. "It hit me. I'm not sure what's wrong, but Peregrine shifted."

Jarvis looked at the people around him. More pack members had arrived, and Frederic was using them to keep the humans away. It meant Jarvis could tell Sam what had happened without fearing someone who shouldn't hear it. It was already dangerous enough for Peregrine to shift and do what he'd done. Jarvis would never forgive himself if he outed the entire pack to the town.

"He took my pain away," he explained, keeping his voice soft.

Sam frowned. "I didn't know he could do that."

"I didn't, either. I thought he could only heal illnesses, but he did it. I'm not in any pain."

Sam grimaced. "Good, because we're going to have to take you back to pack territory before I can heal you. I don't think I should do this in front of so many people."

"It's fine." Or at least, Jarvis hoped it would be. "But someone has to find Peregrine. He needs to be protected. The people who are after him might be able to find him now." And nothing terrified Jarvis more than the thought of losing Peregrine.

Sam nodded. "Okay. Frederic is going to help me put you into our truck. Once you're there, he'll go find Peregrine. I'll drive you back to pack territory."

Jarvis didn't want to leave without Peregrine, but he couldn't tell Sam he wasn't going anywhere. He also couldn't wait for an ambulance to arrive. Who knew what would happen if he was taken to a hospital?

Luckily, by the time Jarvis was in Frederic's truck—in pain again and crying—Peregrine had come back. His expression was grim, but he climbed into the truck next to Jarvis, and, to Jarvis's surprise, he took one of his hands in his and linked their fingers together. "How are you feeling?" he asked.

"Sam says he can heal me, but we have to go back to pack territory first."

Peregrine nodded. "Good. I need to pack my things and leave as soon as possible."

That was what Jarvis had been afraid of. He sucked in a breath and held Peregrine's hand tighter as Frederic and Sam finally climbed into the truck. Sam got in next to Jarvis, and Jarvis looked at him. "I want you to heal me now."

Sam looked startled. "Are you sure? It's probably better if we wait until we're back in pack territory. I don't want to make a mistake and do something wrong."

Jarvis shook his head. "I trust you to do this. Please." Because once they got to pack territory, he had to be there for

Peregrine. He didn't know what would come next, but he hoped that since Cam had known what would happen if Peregrine healed someone, he would offer Peregrine protection. It might not be enough, but it was worth a try.

The problem was that it would only work if Peregrine allowed it and agreed to stay, and Jarvis wasn't sure he would.

CHAPTER THREE

Peregrine was panicking. As soon as they got back to pack territory, he had to get into his bedroom and pack his things. The sooner he was out of here, the sooner he and the pack would be safe.

He barely noticed Sam taking off his seatbelt and climbing into the back seat. He almost landed on Peregrine's lap, which made Peregrine jerk. "What's going on?" he asked.

Sam looked apologetic. "Sorry. Jarvis wants me to heal him."

Peregrine didn't understand. "Shouldn't you wait until we get to pack territory?"

"He wants me to do it now."

Was Jarvis in pain again? If that was the case, Peregrine could shift a second time. He wouldn't be able to fly away to disperse the pain, but maybe Sam could open a window. Hell, it would make more sense for Peregrine to fly to pack territory. He'd be faster, and he wasn't sure he wanted to spend more time with Jarvis.

Because he was losing him. Peregrine was leaving, and Jarvis wasn't. Right when Jarvis needed him the most because of what had happened, Peregrine was abandoning him. It wasn't fair, but then, nothing had ever been fair in Peregrine's life.

Peregrine plastered himself against the truck door to give Sam more space. He'd never seen a unicorn heal anyone, and he was curious. It wasn't easy, because there wasn't much space in the back of the truck, but Sam managed to wiggle himself between the backseat and the front one. Then he raised his hands above Jarvis's legs.

They didn't look good. There was blood on Jarvis's torn jeans, and while Peregrine hadn't looked too closely, he was pretty sure he'd seen bone. He hoped he was wrong and that the healing would be easy, but he couldn't help the feeling that he was going to throw up at the thought of what had happened.

Jarvis had saved him. He hadn't had to, but he'd put himself in the car's path so that Peregrine wouldn't be hurt. Instead of thanking him and being there for him, Peregrine was leaving. He wished things were different, but what could he do? The pack and Jarvis had welcomed him, and he couldn't bring danger to their door, which was what would happen once the people after him found him.

If only he knew who they were. Maybe if he did, he would be able to get away from them. But he suspected more than one group of people were after him. Everyone who knew about him and his ability wanted to get their hands on him, making it hard to identify anyone. Peregrine didn't care who wanted him. He just wanted to be left alone, but that had never happened, and he doubted it ever would.

Sam's hands glowed. Peregrine knew from being told that he glowed, too, when he took the illness away from someone. He'd never noticed it himself, and it was interesting. Sam's expression was tight and focused, even though the road was anything but smooth. He didn't seem to notice when his mate hit potholes. His only focus was Jarvis and healing him.

Peregrine was happy to see that. He didn't want Jarvis to be alone once he left, and he'd been afraid that was what would happen, but Jarvis *wasn't* alone. He had Sam and Sage and a lot of the people in the pack.

But those people had been there before, too, and they hadn't helped. Jarvis had been lonely until Peregrine had arrived, and he would be lonely once Peregrine left.

Peregrine couldn't think about that. He had to focus on keeping Jarvis safe rather than happy.

Jarvis jerked, and Peregrine turned his attention to him. Jarvis's eyes were closed, and his face was flushed. He didn't look in pain exactly, but Peregrine still found himself reaching for him. He wouldn't be able to help with the pain, since he was in his human form, but he wanted Jarvis to remember he wasn't alone.

At least for now.

He gently touched Jarvis's forehead, and Jarvis relaxed. One of his hands reached up, taking Peregrine's. It was the first time Jarvis did something like that. Usually, it was Peregrine who reached for him and who touched him. It felt good but also painful because this was one of the last times Peregrine would have this.

His time in Rosewood was over.

He took Jarvis's hand and squeezed it. Then he focused on Sam, staring at him until Sam's hands stopped glowing and he straightened as much as he could, considering the space they were in. He looked more tired now, with lines on his forehead and dark shadows under his eyes. He still appeared triumphant when he glanced at Peregrine.

"I did what I could. I hope it's fine, but Jarvis, you still should allow the healer to look at you once we get home."

Jarvis opened his eyes. He looked down at his legs, then tentatively moved one of them. It didn't seem to hurt, because he swung both of them to the side and sat up. Sam sighed in relief and sat down into the seat Jarvis had freed while Jarvis turned to Peregrine. He hadn't let go of his hand, and now, he took Peregrine's second hand, too. "You can't go."

Peregrine closed his eyes. He'd known Jarvis wouldn't want him to leave, and he didn't, either. "I have to. I used my ability."

"When I didn't want you to," Jarvis snapped.

He'd never talked to Peregrine that way, and while Peregrine knew why he was angry, he didn't like it. He never wanted Jarvis to be mad at him. "What was I supposed to do? You were in pain, and I could take that pain away. Should I have ignored it?"

"Yes, because I knew this was going to happen. It's why I didn't want you to take the pain away."

"It was the least I could do for you."

Jarvis squeezed Peregrine's hand. "Don't you see? The least you could have done was listen to me. I didn't want you to take the pain away because it was useless, and I knew you'd do it. Don't you think I would rather have you by my side and be in pain than not feel anything and have you leave?"

That was the most Peregrine had ever heard Jarvis say. He didn't like that it was in these circumstances. He wanted to find out more about Jarvis, about what made him tick and what made him happy. He was out of time, though, no matter his wishes and wants.

"We're almost there," Sam murmured. He was trying hard not to stare, but Peregrine didn't miss his looks of pity.

He didn't like pity. He didn't want people to feel that for him, but he supposed it was better than hatred. It would be normal for Sam to dislike Peregrine for bringing danger to the pack. That was why Peregrine wanted to leave before anything happened and the pack realized what was going on. Rosewood was the one place where he'd felt at home since he could remember, and even though he couldn't stay, he didn't want to lose that.

He wanted to remember Rosewood the way it was when he'd been staying here. He wanted to have the illusion that he could come back if he wanted to and that he'd be welcomed with open arms. Nothing could be further from the truth, but it didn't matter.

"Peregrine," Jarvis begged. "Please. Don't do this."

"How can I not? You know what's going to happen if I don't leave, and I won't put you or the pack in danger."

"So you'll put yourself in danger instead?"

Peregrine had to put some distance between them. Even though he could tell it hurt Jarvis from Jarvis's expression, he took his hands away and pushed himself even closer to the door. "I'm used to being in danger. This is nothing new, and just like it happened in the past, it will continue to happen in the future. It's my life, Jarvis. The pack shouldn't have to deal with it, and while I'm grateful for the way you welcomed me, I won't allow anything to happen to you."

Because as long as Peregrine knew Rosewood was safe and Jarvis was here, living his life, he would be fine. He had to be.

Jarvis was losing Peregrine, and he didn't know how to stop it. He understood how much helping him had cost Peregrine, but he still didn't think running away was the best idea. He didn't know how to convince Peregrine of that, and that was a problem. Peregrine was trying to do the right thing, or at least, what he thought was the right thing. He was attempting to keep the pack and Jarvis safe, and while Jarvis was touched, he also was freaking out at the thought of losing Peregrine.

He wanted to ask Peregrine if he really was willing to abandon his mate, but they hadn't talked about it, and he didn't want to do it in front of Sam and Frederic.

He was relieved when they reached pack territory and nothing happened. No one tried to stop the truck, and no one jumped them to get to Peregrine. Cam and Toby were waiting in front of their house when Frederic parked, and they moved toward them right away.

Peregrine was out of the truck before Jarvis could try to stop him. Jarvis scrambled out after Peregrine, who thankfully had been stopped by Cam and Toby, who were checking that he was okay. Peregrine was trying to get past them, but they'd have none of that, and Jarvis hoped it was because they understood what was going on.

Jarvis almost fell on his face. He got to his feet and realized everyone was staring at him, but he didn't even care. He was used to looking like an idiot, and if it helped keep Peregrine here, he would fall out of trucks every day of his life.

"He's planning to leave," he said when he reached the alpha.

Peregrine looked at him as if he'd betrayed him, but Jarvis didn't care. Even if Peregrine hated him and wanted nothing to do with him, Jarvis would know he'd done everything he could to keep Peregrine safe. That was what he had to do, just like Peregrine felt the need to leave.

Cam turned his attention to Peregrine. "Why don't you tell me what happened first?"

That wasn't what Jarvis had hoped to hear, but at least Peregrine wasn't rushing into his bedroom or flying away.

Jarvis looked around the clearing. A few people were on their porches, staring. They were curious, but then, everyone always was. The pack was small, and everyone was all up in everyone else's business.

"I shouldn't be wasting time," Peregrine said. "All you have to know is that I used my ability, which means someone will find me."

Cam and Toby looked at each other. Toby nodded, then reached for Peregrine. "Let's go inside," he murmured. "I'm sure you'll feel less exposed."

"I know you want me to stay, but I can't. I'm a danger for your pack now," Peregrine told him.

"We realize that. We would never kick out a pack member

because he's in danger, though, and that includes you."

Peregrine looked like he didn't understand, but Jarvis's heart felt like it was in his throat. He'd wished Peregrine were part of the pack ever since Peregrine had arrived, but no one had said anything, so it wasn't official. He was relieved to hear that might not be a problem anymore.

Because if Peregrine was part of the pack, the pack would fight for him. They would protect him like they'd protected Sam and Toby, and right now, that was all that mattered.

Jarvis trailed behind the small group. Sam had disappeared, no doubt to find the healer and bring her around so she could check on Jarvis's legs. Jarvis felt fine, but he was afraid to look at his own body, not knowing what he would find if he did. The healing hadn't hurt, but he suspected that was thanks to Peregrine and the pain he'd taken away. Jarvis had no idea how that worked. And while he was grateful because he was a wimp and never dealt well with pain, he was also angry at Peregrine, both for taking away his pain and for ignoring his demand that he not do it.

Now wasn't the time to focus on that.

He followed the other three to Cam's office. He'd never had the opportunity to come here since Cam had become the alpha, but he had when Cam's father was in charge. The place was different, yet it felt the same. It was safe, and Jarvis found himself relaxing.

"Why don't you sit down?" Cam said.

But Peregrine was stubborn, and he stood there, his arms crossed over his chest, shaking his head. "Don't you see? I have to go as soon as possible. I don't have time to sit down."

Cam raised his hands. "All right. You don't have to do anything you don't want to."

"Does that include staying here? Because to me, it looks like you're trying to stop me from leaving, and I don't understand why."

Cam sat in his chair. Toby stood next to him, a hand on his shoulder, which was enough to tell Jarvis that both of them agreed with whatever Cam was about to say. Toby was new to the alpha mate thing, but he was a good person, and Jarvis knew he would do the right thing — whatever the right thing was.

"We knew this would eventually happen," Cam said.

"It always happens," Peregrine snapped.

Cam didn't look offended. "We'll protect you."

"No one can protect me. They always find me, and the only thing I can do is run."

Cam leaned forward. "But you've always been alone. That's why you run, isn't it? Because you're alone, and no one can protect you."

Peregrine's shoulders slumped, and he raked a hand through his hair. "Don't you think I *want* to stay? For once in my life, I was starting to feel like maybe I'd found a home. The last thing I want is to leave, but I can't put you and your pack in danger. It wouldn't be fair, not when I can do what I always do and run away. If you're worried about me, you shouldn't be. I'll be fine. I always am."

Jarvis's heart raced. Peregrine had been fine until now, but if people were going to try to catch him for decades to come, eventually, they'd succeed. What would happen to Peregrine then? He would be imprisoned like he had been when he was a child, and it wasn't fair. No one should have to go through what Peregrine had gone through, and Jarvis would do everything he could to make sure he didn't. He wasn't quite sure what that meant, but he'd found a friend, and he would do whatever needed to be done to keep Peregrine safe.

Even go against Peregrine's wishes.

"Please, think about staying," Cam said. "We *are* worried about you, and we don't want anything to happen to you. We also don't want you to have to run for the rest of your life.

You're only twenty-nine, Peregrine. That could be another fifty years, and I don't think you want that."

"No one would want that. But you can't seriously be choosing me over your pack."

"I don't think the choice is between you and the pack. It's between helping you and allowing you to be rash and leave."

"But don't you see? If they find me, they'll do anything they can to get to me. That includes attacking your pack."

Cam and Toby glanced at each other. "We talked about that," Toby said. "We're aware that's one outcome, but it's not the only one that could happen. Besides, the pack is stronger now. We have the twins, and that's usually enough to keep most people away."

"They might be phoenix shifters, but they can't work miracles."

"We're not saying they can. I doubt an army will be sent to find you, though, especially not right now. Even if a few people arrive looking for you, we'll be able to defend you.

"We consider you part of the pack, even though we've never talked about it. More importantly, we promised to keep you safe when you healed Basil, and we have every intention of keeping that promise. Why don't you give it a try? Stay for a few days and see what happens."

Peregrine still didn't look convinced. Jarvis didn't think it was his place to intervene, but he had to. "Stay for me," he blurted out.

Everyone turned to look at him. He could feel his cheeks flush, but he didn't care. He looked straight at Peregrine, focusing only on him. "Please. Stay for me. You're the best friend I've ever had, and I don't want to lose you, especially not for helping me. I realize it's selfish, but Toby and Cam are right. You can't run for the rest of your life, and the pack will protect you. See what happens. Stay with me for a few days. Please." Jarvis wasn't beyond begging if it kept Peregrine with him.

Peregrine wanted to say yes and mean it, but how could he? No matter how much he wanted to stay, no matter that he knew Cam and Toby were right and he couldn't run for the rest of his life, he wouldn't put the pack and Jarvis in danger.

The three of them would push until Peregrine said yes, though, so he nodded. He would find a way to leave the pack before things got too bad. He had to. The best thing right now was to smooth things over as well as he could. Then later, when he was alone and able to, he'd pack his things and sneak out. No one would notice, and he'd be safe.

"All right," he said. The words tasted like ash on his tongue, but he ignored that and focused on the good he was doing.

He was lying to Jarvis, something he'd never wanted to do, but the only thing he *could* do. Jarvis would be hurt when he found out Peregrine had left during the night, but it was something Peregrine was willing to deal with. It was something he would *have* to deal with, but for now, he was keeping Jarvis safe, and that was all that mattered.

Jarvis blinked at him. "All right?"

"I'm staying," Peregrine agreed. "I don't think it's a smart idea, but you're right. I can't continue running for the rest of my life, and I don't wish to. I like the pack, and I want to stay. I'll give it a try and see what happens. I can't promise I won't ever leave, but for now, I'll stay."

Jarvis's shoulders slumped.

That had to be from relief, which made Peregrine feel guilty. He had to remember that no matter how much he hurt Jarvis, he was doing it to keep him safe. Jarvis would understand that eventually, and even if he didn't, Peregrine would be far away.

This was the only way Cam and Jarvis would back down from trying to convince him to stay. He might have been able to persuade Toby it was for the best, although he wasn't sure about that, either. Toby usually stood with Cam when it came to these things. Even though Peregrine hadn't been here for long, he already knew that.

He rubbed his face. "I need some sleep."

Jarvis looked guilty. "Because you healed me."

"I didn't heal you. I just took away the pain, but yes. That's why I need rest."

"Why don't you go to your room? I'll get some food together, and I'll bring it to you," Toby said. His gaze moved to Jarvis. "You can stay if you want."

"I should probably go home, if anything, to shower and change." Jarvis looked down at his legs. "And I'm sure Naila will want to check my legs."

"Peregrine is safe here," Toby promised. "Go home. You can come back anytime you want, although maybe it would be best if you waited until tomorrow. Peregrine needs sleep."

Peregrine did his best to ignore the heavy guilt in his chest. He nodded when Jarvis looked at him, and even though he wanted to step away when Jarvis moved closer, he didn't. He'd promised he'd stay, and he was going to break that promise, but he needed everyone to believe he wouldn't. That included Jarvis.

When Jarvis took his hand, Peregrine almost started crying. His eyes burned, and he wanted to throw himself into Jarvis's arms and never let go. He wanted to believe Jarvis could protect him, but he knew better.

"I'm glad you agree to stay," Jarvis murmured. He hesitated, then, to Peregrine's surprise, kissed Peregrine's cheek. "I know this isn't easy for you. I'll see you tomorrow morning?"

Peregrine nodded. "You need to get some rest, too. I know

Sam healed you, but you still lost some blood, and your body went through a shock. Take care of yourself." Because Peregrine wouldn't be there to take care of him.

Jarvis stared for a moment before nodding. "I will. And you have to take care of yourself."

"I will." And of the pack and Jarvis. Taking care of them meant leaving.

Toby walked Jarvis to the front door while Cam took Peregrine to his room. He didn't step in, instead pausing at the door. "Toby will bring you some food. You should take a shower and get into bed."

Peregrine swallowed. He couldn't sneak out until tonight, which meant he had time for a nap and food, as well as for packing. This way, no one would realize what he was doing until it was too late. When Cam and Toby woke up tomorrow morning, he would be far away, and they wouldn't be able to find him.

Cam turned to leave, but Peregrine found himself stopping him. "Thank you," he said.

Cam smiled. "What are you thanking me for?"

"No one has ever offered me protection the way you did. I can't believe you're willing to sacrifice the pack's safety for me, and I don't understand it, but thank you. It means everything."

Cam stared at Peregrine until Peregrine was afraid that he would see right through him. Thankfully, that was impossible, and Cam nodded. "I know you're afraid, and that trouble is coming. We'll do everything we can to protect you. You healed Basil, and you helped Jarvis. More importantly, you've been staying with us for a while now, and everyone considers you part of the family. Toby would kick my ass if I didn't do this for you."

Peregrine waited until Cam had walked away to enter his bedroom. He looked around, and one tear finally fell.

He'd thought he'd finally found a home. He hadn't wanted to believe it, to hope, and he was right, but in the many years he'd been on the run, this was the hardest time yet. It was the one time he had so much to leave behind. He didn't know what would hurt more — losing Jarvis or losing the pack and the feeling of belonging to something. He didn't think it mattered. It would hurt either way.

He was going to miss Rosewood and the pack, especially Jarvis. Peregrine had thought he would finally be able to settle down, and he would have if he hadn't taken the pain away from Jarvis. He didn't regret it, even though it meant he was on the run again. Jarvis had saved him from the car, and it was the least Peregrine could do. He would have done it even if Jarvis hadn't saved him, though. He was in love with Jarvis, and that feeling would have been enough for him to do everything he could.

That included leaving. Jarvis was probably going to hate him after this, but Peregrine had no choice.

He sighed and headed to the bathroom. He wanted a shower. He'd try to find a motel somewhere for tomorrow night, but he had to put as much distance as he could between himself and Rosewood, so it would probably be best if he stayed on the run for the next few days and, more importantly, stayed out of sight. Everything depended on what would happen once he started running.

But since he was staying here for the rest of today, he would take advantage of it. Maybe if he tried hard enough, he could ignore the heavy weight of reality and act as if he was home. He wouldn't be able to do it for long, but he needed a few moments to feel like he still belonged.

He managed to keep the tears in as he showered, but they freely fell when he went back to the bedroom and found a plate with a sandwich on the dresser. There was also a bottle of water and a slice of pie, and he found himself sobbing in front of them, realizing how much he would lose this time and how much he didn't want to go.

These people truly cared for him, even though he didn't understand why. He'd always kept everyone away because he hadn't wanted to go through this, and now, he remembered why. Leaving people he cared about behind hurt too much, and he promised himself this was the last time he would do this.

His heart wouldn't stand it a second time.

Contrary to what most people thought, Jarvis wasn't an idiot. Peregrine had given in way too easily when he'd agreed to stay, which had made Jarvis suspicious. He'd gone home just like he'd said he would. He'd showered, had eaten something, and had even taken a nap after Naila declared him healed. But he'd brushed off his mother when she'd asked what had happened, and he hadn't stayed for dinner. He couldn't because he didn't want to risk Peregrine slipping past him.

He'd been hiding in the bushes outside Cam's house since dinner time, and so far, nothing weird happened. Jarvis was convinced Peregrine was going to run away, so he stayed right where he was, even though his legs and butt hurt – and it had nothing to do with the car hitting him. The ground was uncomfortable, and he wished he had a pillow.

He leaned the back of his head against the tree he was sitting next to and watched the window he knew belonged to Peregrine's room. It was dark, which most people would have believed meant Peregrine was asleep, but Jarvis knew he wasn't. No matter how meek Peregrine had acted with Cam and Toby, he was going to try something, and he was going to try it tonight. He took the need to protect the pack seriously, which meant he wasn't going to stick around to see what happened. He couldn't allow it, not when he'd been through this so many times already.

Jarvis sighed. That wasn't a life for anyone, but especially not for Peregrine. It wasn't fair that he had to go through something like this again and again, and Jarvis wanted Peregrine to know he wasn't alone. If he had to, he would follow him to the end of the world, which was why he'd also packed a backpack.

It wasn't like Jarvis had a lot to leave behind. He would miss his family, but then, maybe he wouldn't. He loved them, and he knew they loved him, but they'd never gotten along well. He would miss the pack, but he wasn't close to any pack member, so even that wouldn't be much. He could find another job at any coffee shop in the country, and he had some money put aside, so he and Peregrine could find a cheap apartment or something like that.

That was, if Peregrine allowed Jarvis to go with him. Jarvis wouldn't take no for an answer, but he didn't know if Peregrine would be on foot or wing. If he shifted into his caladrius form, it would be a problem for Jarvis. Even if he shifted into his wolf form, it would be too easy for him to lose Peregrine as he flew. But Peregrine had a backpack, and even though he didn't own many things, the things he did own were precious to him. He wouldn't leave them behind, no matter how much of a rush he was in. There was no way for him to carry the backpack if he was in his bird form, so Jarvis hoped it meant he would be on foot.

Something moved in the house, and Jarvis turned his attention back to it. He held his breath, hoping he wasn't about to see Cam naked through the window or something like that. He didn't like spying on people, especially not the alpha, but this was the only way he'd found to make sure he knew what Peregrine was up to.

No light came on inside the house, but Peregrine's window

slowly opened. Jarvis stared as a slight figure climbed out the window after throwing a backpack through it. He'd known Peregrine was going to do this, and he was angry at him, but now wasn't the moment to yell at him. He would make sure to do it later.

Jarvis tried to stay as silent as he could. He'd never done anything like this, but Peregrine was in a rush and probably freaking out. He moved quickly, so quickly it was hard for Jarvis to keep up, but Peregrine never noticed Jarvis walking behind him.

They stuck to the forest as they moved toward the town. Jarvis hoped Peregrine wasn't going to try to find a bus or something like that, but he doubted there would be anything available at this hour of the night. It was going on two AM, and Peregrine wouldn't risk staying in Rosewood. That meant walking away, which, thankfully, was what Peregrine did.

Once he reached Rosewood, he walked down Main Street until he reached the edge of town. Then he continued.

He almost noticed Jarvis a few times while they were in Rosewood, but once they were out of town, it became easier to follow him without being noticed. There were more places to hide, and Jarvis took advantage of them as much as he could.

He didn't know how long they walked. He didn't look at the time, not caring. They continued walking until the sky started to lighten, though, and he hoped they were going to stop soon. He was afraid that if they didn't, Peregrine would notice him, but of course, he wasn't the one making that decision. If Peregrine went on, Jarvis would, too.

By the time they stopped, Jarvis couldn't feel his feet anymore. They ached something fierce, and he was so relieved he almost fell on his knees. That would get Peregrine's attention, so he didn't.

Peregrine stopped at a motel. He walked into the office, not once looking behind himself, and Jarvis felt better at having been able to hide as he followed Peregrine.

Then, he realized he wouldn't be sleeping in the motel room with Peregrine. If anything, he would have to sleep outside so he could be sure Peregrine wouldn't sneak away by the time night fell again.

Jarvis groaned. Thankfully, he'd packed some food in his backpack, but it wouldn't last him long. Besides, eventually he was going to have to tell Peregrine he was following him. He wasn't looking forward to that, and Peregrine would be pissed, but Jarvis wasn't planning on following Peregrine for the rest of his life. What he wanted was to be with him, even if it was only as a friend, and to protect him. That was why he'd left the pack and why he wasn't turning around, no matter what Peregrine said or did.

Jarvis looked around. They weren't in Rosewood anymore, and there wasn't a tree in sight. It wasn't what Jarvis was used to, and it made his skin feel itchy, but since Peregrine wasn't going to take long inside the office, he hid behind a car. From where he was, he could see Peregrine, and hopefully, he'd be able to find out what room Peregrine was sleeping in. He had to do everything he could to be in sight of that room so he'd know when Peregrine left.

A handful of minutes later, Peregrine came out of the office, holding a key. Thankfully, his room was on the ground floor, and Jarvis was able to hide behind cars as he followed him toward it. Peregrine disappeared inside the room, and Jarvis sat behind the car closest to it. He leaned his head against the trunk, wondering what now. He was pretty sure someone would notice if he sat there for the entire day, but things might get worse if he shifted. He was a wolf, after all. People wouldn't allow him to hang around just because he was cute. But first he wanted to eat something. Then maybe he could take his shoes off, at least for a bit. He was almost afraid to look at his feet.

He took one of his sandwiches out of the backpack and stuffed it into his mouth. He was still chewing when he felt something move next to him, but by the time he turned around, it was too late.

Peregrine was standing there, his hands on his hips, looking pissed. "What the fuck are you doing here?" he demanded to know.

CHAPTER FOUR

Peregrine was still pissed that evening. He'd been tempted to send Jarvis back to the pack right away, but Jarvis had been hit by a car yesterday, and even though he'd been an idiot and had followed Peregrine, he needed rest.

Peregrine twisted in his chair and looked at Jarvis, who was asleep in the bed. Peregrine had ordered him to get some rest after they'd talked, and while Jarvis had protested, he'd fallen asleep as soon as his head had touched the pillow. That meant Peregrine had spent the night in a chair and his back hurt, but it was only for one night. Tonight, he *would* send Jarvis back to the pack, and he wouldn't hear anything about Jarvis staying, no matter what Jarvis had been trying to convince him of this morning.

Peregrine couldn't believe it. He hadn't thought anyone had realized he was planning to sneak out, but then he hadn't thought Jarvis knew him so well. He'd told Peregrine he'd known what Peregrine would do, which was why he'd waited under his window. He'd followed him all the way to this motel, and Peregrine wasn't sure what to make of it.

On the one hand, he was pleased. People had never come after him. They'd dismissed him as soon as he left, and he didn't blame them. No one had cared enough to worry about him and what he was doing except for Jarvis, and it made Peregrine want to take Jarvis with him, especially considering their bond.

But he couldn't. It was too dangerous, and besides, Jarvis had a life and a family in Rosewood. It wasn't right for him to be on the run, especially when he didn't need to.

And then, Peregrine was terrified. What if the people after him found him and Jarvis was with him? It could happen at any second, and it made him want to wake Jarvis up and kick him out now while they were still safe. The problem was that Jarvis wouldn't stand for that. Apparently, Peregrine was the one person he stood up to, and while Peregrine would have been proud of that in any other situation, it complicated things in this one.

Jarvis groaned and turned. He flopped onto his back, and his eyes opened. He raised one hand and rubbed his face, then sat up.

He was still wearing his clothes. Peregrine had told him to make himself comfortable when he'd sent him to bed this morning, but he hadn't wanted to undress, and Peregrine wasn't sure if it was because he didn't want to risk it in case someone found them or because he didn't want Peregrine to see him in any kind of undress.

"Good morning," Jarvis said.

Peregrine glared at him from his chair. "It's evening," he snapped.

Jarvis's tentative smile fell. "You're still angry."

Peregrine shot to his feet, but there was nowhere for him to go, so he paced the room instead. "Of course I'm pissed. Do you understand what you did?"

Jarvis crossed his arms over his chest. "Do you understand what *you* did?"

"I tried to keep you and the pack safe. With me gone, the people after me won't come to Rosewood. But you're with me, which means you're in danger. You have to go back."

"I'm not going anywhere."

Peregrine huffed. Until as recently as yesterday, Jarvis would have done anything Peregrine asked of him. Peregrine had known that, and he'd tried his best not to take advantage of it. But now that it was important Jarvis do what Peregrine asked, he wasn't budging. Peregrine was glad Jarvis was standing up for himself, but it complicated an already tricky situation.

The fact that Peregrine was also touched made everything worse. No one had ever come after him when he'd left a place. No one had cared enough. But there was no place for Jarvis in his life, even with the bond, and that was a problem. Jarvis had a whole life to go back to, while Peregrine's life consisted of running. Jarvis shouldn't have to do the same, especially when he didn't have a reason to.

Peregrine had tried telling Jarvis that this morning, but Jarvis hadn't seemed to care. Maybe now that he'd had some sleep, he would.

Peregrine came to stand at the foot of the bed. "You can't stay with me."

Jarvis sighed. "Are we going through this again? I thought we'd already talked ourselves out this morning."

"Keep your mouth shut and listen." But Peregrine was trying hard not to smile. "I'm on the run. I've always been on the run, so I know what's going to happen. I'm going to move from motel to motel until they find me. When they do, I'm going to manage to fly away before they catch me, but it's going to be close, and I'm probably going to lose everything I own. Then, I'm going to start again from the beginning. Do you really want your life to be that?"

Jarvis stared at Peregrine. "What if they manage to catch you?"

"They never do." But it was a fear Peregrine lived with every day of his life, and he didn't want Jarvis to have to do the same. "This isn't a life for you, Jarvis. You have a home, a job, and you could have friends if you allowed them into your life. Go back to Rosewood and be happy."

"I don't think being constantly on the run is a life for you, either," Jarvis said softly. "It's not a life for anyone, and you don't want this."

"Of course I don't. No one would want this. I can't change what my life is like, no matter how much I try. You can. You don't have to do this, and I don't want you to do it. Go back home. You'll forget about me soon enough."

Jarvis glared. It wasn't an expression Peregrine usually saw directed his way, not from Jarvis. "I won't forget about you. You're my best friend, and I don't care what you think or say. I'm not going anywhere unless you come with me."

Peregrine threw his hands in the air. "When did you become so stubborn?"

"When we became friends. When I realized that you really liked me and that you were trying to protect me. When I found out we were mates. Why don't you allow *me* to protect *you* for once?"

It was tempting. Peregrine was selfish enough to want Jarvis around, and he could see he wasn't going to change Jarvis's mind. The best thing he could do was go back to Rosewood so Jarvis went back, too, then leave without Jarvis noticing.

But that wasn't what Peregrine would do. He was a selfish asshole, and he suspected that once Jarvis realized what his life was like, he would want to go home, even without him. Peregrine just had to show him how awful living like this was.

"Fine. You can come with me," he said.

Jarvis's eyes widened. "Really?"

"But you have to keep up with me. And if I tell you to run, you have to do it. It means someone is after us, and I can't risk you."

"I told you I'd protect you."

"But you can't. Trust me. I know these people. They won't let anything get in their way to get their hands on me, and that includes hurting you or anyone else who puts themselves in their path. The only reason I'm agreeing to you coming with me is that I know you won't go back, no matter how many times I asked. That means I have to keep you safe, as well as keeping myself safe. It's not going to be easy." But Peregrine was willing to do it.

He was willing to do a lot to keep Jarvis safe and to have him with him. He wouldn't last long anyway, because Peregrine had no doubt he'd want to go home once he realized how hard this was.

Jarvis shot out of bed, but his legs were tangled in the blanket, and he fell on his face. Peregrine briefly closed his eyes. His heart felt like it was about to explode with affection and love, and it was hard to deal with.

He loved Jarvis. He'd never seen it coming because if he had, he would have stayed away from him. He hadn't, and now, their lives were entangled. Until he found a way to separate them without hurting Jarvis even more than he already had, Peregrine would have to take care of him.

No matter what Jarvis thought, he wasn't equipped to deal with whatever was about to happen. The problem was that Peregrine couldn't see a way to leave Jarvis behind without breaking both their hearts.

Jarvis suspected Peregrine was planning something, no doubt to send him back to Rosewood. He'd meant what he'd said, though. He wasn't going anywhere unless Peregrine went with him, and that included back home.

Jarvis hadn't turned his phone on since he'd left home yesterday. He knew his mother, at the very least, had to be frantic because she couldn't find him, and she'd probably gone to Cam, who would know what had happened. They would have no way to find out where Jarvis and Peregrine were, and Jarvis wanted things that way, at least for now.

He knew what his mom would do if she found out where he was. She'd try to convince him to come home, and if he didn't, she'd come to get him. She didn't care that he was an adult or that at twenty-six, he could make his own decisions. That included running after Peregrine when Peregrine left Rosewood. She wouldn't see things that way, but Jarvis didn't care. He would have come even if Peregrine hadn't been his mate, but he was, even though they still hadn't talked about it.

"Are you ready?" Peregrine asked, looking at Jarvis.

Jarvis looked around the motel room. They'd packed everything into their backpacks, so there was no sign that they had spent any length of time here. It was the same as it had been when they'd arrived yesterday.

He looked at Peregrine again. "I am."

Peregrine's expression was grim, but he opened the motel door and stepped outside.

Jarvis followed. He would follow Peregrine everywhere, no matter what Peregrine thought. He wasn't going to stop trying to send Jarvis back home, but for once, Jarvis was planning on doing what he wanted instead of what others told him to do.

"What did you tell your parents?" Peregrine asked.

Jarvis didn't know where they were headed, but he followed his best friend down the street. Peregrine seemed to know what he was doing, which he probably did since he'd been on the run since he was fourteen.

Jarvis couldn't imagine living like this for fifteen years. It wasn't fair, and he wanted Peregrine to go back to Rosewood and have the life he'd always wanted. Peregrine didn't think he could have it, but maybe Jarvis would manage to convince him in time. Finding out who was after him and convincing them to stop would help, but Jarvis doubted that would ever happen.

"I didn't tell them anything," he answered.

Peregrine frowned. "What do you mean?"

"I left through the window like you did. I told them I was tired after being hit by that car and went to bed. Mom brought me dinner, but I didn't see her again after she picked up the plate. She thought she was going to find me in the room this morning."

Peregrine stopped moving. "Are you seriously telling me you ran away from home?"

Jarvis bristled. "I'm twenty-six. I didn't run away from home. I decided to leave."

Peregrine looked like he wanted to strangle Jarvis, which Jarvis thought was entirely possible. "You didn't tell them what was going on. You didn't tell them that you were leaving."

"Of course not. They would have tried to stop me, and when I didn't, they would have contacted Cam. I couldn't do that to you."

Peregrine stared. "I don't know whether I should kiss you or slap you."

Jarvis's face felt like it went up in flames, but Peregrine wasn't done.

"I don't understand how you can care so much more about me than you care about yourself or your family. We've known each other for weeks, yet you're putting me before everything and everyone else in your life."

"Because you deserve it."

"Why? I didn't do anything."

This wasn't something Jarvis wanted to talk about, especially with Peregrine. If he wanted this to work, though, he needed to be honest. "You accepted me the way I am. You didn't try to change me, to tell me I should buy better-looking clothes or that I should find a better job. You didn't tell me I needed to lose weight."

"I can't believe that everyone else has been telling you those things. Toby wouldn't have. Neither would Sam or Sage or Basil."

"I don't know them well, but I agree."

"You could be their friend."

Maybe Jarvis could. They'd seemed friendly enough at the coffee shop, but he'd never approached them. They were special, while he was just Jarvis. What would they do with someone like him in their life? Jarvis still didn't understand what Peregrine saw in him, but he'd stopped trying. It no doubt had to do with the bond. "But I'm yours instead, and I intend to stay your friend. That means following you and keeping you safe."

"You could get hurt." Peregrine's voice was soft and hesitant.

He'd been angry until now, but Jarvis could see his fear. He didn't want anything to happen to him, something else Jarvis wasn't used to. His parents had always been more worried about his siblings than they were for him. He was just Jarvis. He would never do anything to put himself in trouble, would he?

Except he had. His mother had to be frantic by now, and he was tempted to turn on his phone to find out.

"I could get hurt," he agreed. "So could you. That hasn't stopped you."

"Because I've known I could get hurt for the past fifteen years. Because I've *been* hurt, and I survived."

"I'll survive, too."

"But you shouldn't have to! You don't have a reason to be here. No one is coming after you, and you should go home to Rosewood and live your life. You can't abandon everything for me, not when you barely know me."

"I know you enough to care about you. What am I leaving behind? A job I can do in pretty much every town in the country. Parents who barely care about me."

"I'm sure they love you."

"And I love them. It doesn't mean we're close, and I don't think we'll ever be."

"What about the pack? Cam cares about you, and so do the others. They're going to be frantic not knowing what happened to you."

"I think they know what happened to me. And yes, Cam cares. He cares about everyone in the pack, which makes sense since he's the alpha." Jarvis looked around to make sure no one was listening, but it was late and the street was almost empty. Only a few people walked quickly on the sidewalks, clearly needing to be somewhere. "And yes, I realize he's probably worried, but he's worried about you as well. No matter what you try to convince yourself of, you became a pack member when you arrived in Rosewood. That means Cam is responsible for both of us, not only for me."

And *that* was why Peregrine should have stayed in Rosewood. Jarvis wished he had. It wasn't only because he didn't like this being on the run business. It was also because he'd watched Peregrine over the weeks he'd spent in town. He'd slowly relaxed and had started to feel at home. Jarvis was ready to bet it was the only time Peregrine had felt that way, and he didn't want the man he loved to lose that.

Peregrine could have the life he'd always wanted if he stayed in Rosewood. It wouldn't be easy, and he would have to face his past and the people after him, but it would be better for him to be with a group of people who would do everything to keep him safe than being on his own traveling the country.

Except he wasn't on his own anymore. Jarvis was with him, and he prayed he wouldn't make a mess out of this. He had no experience fighting, and he would probably die the first time they were attacked, but as long as it gave Peregrine time to run away, he would die in peace.

Jarvis wasn't a martyr. He didn't *want* to die. But for the first time, he was ready to do anything to help someone, and that included losing his life. It was terrifying, but it was important.

Peregrine was important.

Peregrine thought about what Jarvis had said as they walked. He was still angry, both because Jarvis had put himself in danger and because he refused to go home, but also at himself for allowing this to happen. The problem was that he was also relieved not to be alone.

Peregrine had been alone all his life. Even when he'd lived with the old man in the beginning, they hadn't been close. The old man had only needed Peregrine to heal him because he was sick, and as soon as Peregrine did it, he went back to his rooms. He'd been comfortable and had everything he could have wanted as a child, but he'd been lonely.

And after the old man had died, things had turned worse. The man who had taken him on then hadn't cared about keeping Peregrine happy. He only cared about what Peregrine could do and for how much he could sell that, and he hadn't hesitated to hit Peregrine when Peregrine had something to say about it. Peregrine had been alone then, too, but he'd been relieved because it meant he could run away.

And he had. For fifteen years, he'd been running, always alone. He'd yearned for human contact, for someone to call a friend, maybe more. He'd found all of that in Jarvis, but now that he had, he wished he hadn't.

If he and Jarvis hadn't become friends — if they weren't mates — Jarvis wouldn't be here right now. He would be safe at home, with his family, and eventually, he would find his way in life. He hadn't yet, and he thought it was an impossible task, but he was young. He had all the time in the world to find out what he wanted and to obtain it, and it wasn't fair that Peregrine was dragging him all over the country with people running after them.

Jarvis was Peregrine's weakness. Peregrine had many of those, but none of the others was a person. He didn't know what he was doing when it came to Jarvis, and he wasn't used to any of this.

He'd been with people, usually in clubs and bars. None of them had been like Jarvis. Hell, Peregrine hadn't known the names of most of them. He hadn't wanted to know because he hadn't wanted to take the risk of getting close to anyone. Yet he'd allowed Jarvis in, and he still didn't understand why he had. He wanted to blame it on the bond between them, but he didn't think that was the reason, not entirely.

It was a problem. Peregrine couldn't allow anything to happen to Jarvis, but he didn't know if he could keep him safe. He was going to try his hardest, but was it enough?

"Where are we going?" Jarvis asked.

"I don't know. I never know where I'm going when I'm on the run."

"Are we going to have to walk all night again?"

There was something in Jarvis's voice that made Peregrine want to smile. He didn't. Instead, he pressed his lips together, but he did peek at Jarvis. He looked like a kicked puppy, and Peregrine could only imagine how much his feet and legs hurt, especially after being hit by a car.

Peregrine sighed. He could never say no to Jarvis, could he? "We can take a bus tonight."

Jarvis's expression brightened. "Really? Where to?"

"We'll see when we get to the station."

They had to walk to the next town over to find one, and when they did, Jarvis was obviously tired. Peregrine didn't ask him how he was or tell him that was one of the reasons he shouldn't stick around. Instead, he picked the first bus out of town, bought both of them a ticket, and dragged Jarvis onto it.

Thankfully, it was late at night, which meant that Jarvis stayed mostly silent as they rode the bus. The people around them were sleeping, but Jarvis wasn't. He and Peregrine had slept most of the day, and Peregrine wasn't tired. He imagined the same went for Jarvis.

Jarvis seemed content to just be with Peregrine. He leaned against Peregrine's side, and Peregrine didn't push him away. He didn't want to. If anything, he wanted to drag Jarvis closer, but doing that would make everything worse. Right now, Peregrine still had the possibility of convincing Jarvis to go back home. Soon Jarvis would realize how hard this kind of life was. He would miss his bed at home, even his family. He would want to go back, and maybe, Peregrine would have a chance to convince him to do just that. If he allowed anything to happen between them, though, he would never get rid of Jarvis.

They arrived so early in the morning that the sky was still dark. Peregrine looked around once they got off the bus, knowing he needed to feed Jarvis. Then they would have to find a place to stay. Peregrine had enough money for a motel, although that money would eventually disappear. It would be a rude awakening for Jarvis, but maybe that was what he needed. Peregrine wanted to enjoy not being alone for a few more days, though, so he would splurge for tonight.

"Let's get something to eat," he said, tilting his chin toward a diner.

It was open and similar to every other diner in the country. Peregrine had visited so many of them that they blurred in his memories. He always got the same food, and today wasn't any different, but Jarvis hesitated.

Peregrine had to look away so Jarvis wouldn't see him

smile. What was it about him that charmed Peregrine the way he did? Peregrine didn't know, but he did know that was one of the reasons he'd always kept people at arm's length. He hadn't wanted something like this to happen. He hadn't been willing to leave people he cared about behind when he had to run, and this showed him what happened when people cared about him. They weren't willing to let him go, and they got themselves in trouble.

"I'm starving," Jarvis said once the food was in front of them. He didn't wait for Peregrine to answer before stuffing a piece of toast into his mouth.

They were silent as they ate. Peregrine had nothing else to say, not when Jarvis wouldn't listen to him. Jarvis, on the other hand, was too busy eating. He cleaned his plate, and when he saw that Peregrine still had food, he looked at him. Peregrine nodded and pushed his plate toward Jarvis, knowing he wouldn't be able to eat anything else. Jarvis's cheeks flushed, but he took the food with a smile and a murmured *thanks*.

Peregrine was ready to sleep when they got to the motel. It was next to the bus station, which meant that they could get another bus later today, and maybe they would manage to reach a city. Cities were a favorite place for Peregrine to stay because they allowed him to lose himself in the crowd.

Peregrine got the first shower, and when he came out, he told Jarvis it was his turn. He could see Jarvis hesitate, and it took him a moment to realize why.

"I'm not going to run while you're in the shower," he said.

Jarvis shrugged without looking at Peregrine. "I want to believe you."

Peregrine sighed. "But you can't because I lied to you and ran away even when I told you and the others I wasn't going to."

Jarvis grimaced but nodded. "I'm sorry. I wish things were

different."

Peregrine shook his head. "They're not, and it's my fault. I don't blame you." He bit his lower lip. "You don't have a reason to trust me, but I swear I'm not going anywhere." He forced himself to smile. "You'd find me anyway, wouldn't you?"

Jarvis grinned. "Probably."

"You really should shower. We don't know when we'll next have the opportunity. We won't always be able to find motels to stay in, you know."

Jarvis grimaced but nodded. "All right. I'll shower."

"And I'll be here when you're done." Because no matter how much Peregrine wished for Jarvis to go home, he never wanted to lie to him again. Jarvis was his best friend, the only man Peregrine had ever loved. It hurt not to reach for him, not to pull him closer and hug him. Peregrine wanted to do all of that, but it would push them even closer than they already were, and Jarvis would take it as a sign he should stay with Peregrine, whatever happened.

Peregrine couldn't allow that. Jarvis had to go home as soon as possible, even though it would break both their hearts.

Jarvis was tempted to keep the bathroom door slightly open to hear if Peregrine snuck out, but he wanted to believe Peregrine. He'd promised, and this time Jarvis thought he meant it. He wasn't going to run away. He might not have accepted that Jarvis wasn't going anywhere, but for now, they were stuck together, and Peregrine knew it. It would be up to Jarvis to make him see he wasn't going home, no matter what happened.

Besides, Jarvis wasn't sure how he would react if Peregrine happened to see him naked.

That wasn't something that appealed to him. He wanted to see Peregrine naked, but he could do without Peregrine seeing him. Even when he'd had boyfriends, he'd made sure to stay half-dressed when they had sex. It didn't matter how many times they said they didn't care. It wasn't like he had a lot of experience with guys anyway. His boyfriends could be counted on one hand, and counting the ones he'd actually had sex with only took two fingers.

Not that he thought he and Peregrine would have sex, even though they were mates. Peregrine needed a friend, and Jarvis didn't want to scare him or send him running a second time. He would keep his feelings to himself. He wasn't blind, and he knew there was no way Peregrine would want more than friendship. He would have said something more about their bond if he had.

But now wasn't the time to think about that. Jarvis quickly stripped and stepped into the shower. The hot water felt good on his back and legs. He couldn't believe how much his entire body ached, especially since he and Peregrine had been sitting in a bus for the whole night. Maybe that was why his back hurt so much. Even though he didn't do any kind of exercise or sport, he was on his feet most of the day at work. He wasn't used to sitting around on a bus for hours at a time.

A loud bang made him jump. He slipped and reached for the shower curtain even though he knew he would pull it down with his body. Sure enough, that was what happened. Jarvis's ass hit the shower floor, and he yelped at the pain. The curtain floated down and landed on top of him, and with the water still coming down from the showerhead, it almost suffocated him.

He pushed it away and got out of the shower, trembling but ready to run if something had happened. He wanted to call out to Peregrine, but if someone was here, hopefully they hadn't heard all the noise he'd just made in the bathroom. He might be the only element of surprise that would save Peregrine, and he wasn't willing to sacrifice that just to make himself feel better. Besides, if nothing had happened and Peregrine was just chilling on the bed watching TV, Jarvis didn't want to look overprotective and like he didn't trust Peregrine.

He held his breath and moved closer to the bathroom door. He should have left it open, dammit.

There was shuffling in the bedroom. Then something heavy hit the wall just outside the bathroom. Jarvis jerked back, terrified, but he couldn't stay in the bathroom, not when someone was trying to take Peregrine away. He was here to protect Peregrine and make him feel like he wasn't alone in the world, which included this kind of situation.

Jarvis wasn't a fighter. Even when he'd playfully wrestled with his brothers when they were kids, he'd always lost. This fight wasn't one he could avoid, so he shifted, needing to be ready for anything and to have his fangs and claws at his advantage.

Then he looked at the door. He couldn't open it in his wolf form.

Jarvis shifted again, took a deep breath, slowly opened the door, and shifted once more. Peregrine cried out just then, and Jarvis threw himself out of the bathroom. Instead of opening the door, he almost closed it again, but he was frantic and needed to get to Peregrine, and that seemed to be enough to power him forward.

Peregrine was on his stomach on one of the beds, his legs dangling down as a man pushed him down onto the mattress. Peregrine's arms were behind his back, and the man was trying to tie his wrists. There was another man by the door, and Jarvis hesitated. The most important thing to do now was to free Peregrine, so he threw himself at the guy attempting to tie him up.

Both of the guys had heard Jarvis, but he moved quickly

enough that they didn't have time to react. He was heavy as a wolf, just like he was as a human, and his weight was enough to throw the man off Peregrine. Once Peregrine was free, he scrambled to his feet and pressed his back against the wall, looking at what was happening in the bedroom.

Jarvis didn't have time to ask him if he was okay. Now that Peregrine was free and Jarvis was taking care of one of the guys attacking him, hopefully, he wouldn't get captured.

"What the fuck?" the man by the door asked.

Jarvis focused on the other one since he was still on top of him. He didn't want to kill the guy—he didn't think he would be able to live with himself if he did something like that—so he bit down on the guy's arm. The guy screamed, and blood spurted in Jarvis's mouth. It made Jarvis want to gag, but he tightened his hold until he felt the bone break in his jaw.

That was even worse, and Jarvis let go. By then, the other guy had moved toward them, and Jarvis twisted and growled at him. The guy looked from Jarvis to Peregrine, who was still standing by the wall.

"We just want him. I don't know who the fuck you are, and I don't care. Let us take him, and nothing will happen to you," the man said.

Jarvis threw himself at the man. This time he couldn't take the guy by surprise, but he didn't need to. The guy tried to shift, but he wasn't fast enough, and when Jarvis landed against him, he pushed both of them against the wall. The guy took the brunt of the hit, his head making a hole in the wall. Jarvis smelled blood, although that might have been from what he still had in his mouth.

He backed away and grabbed the man's ankle in his jaw. This time it was easier for him to crunch the bone, but he couldn't believe he'd managed to do it without the guy trying to stop him. The man was still screaming by the time Jarvis backed away and toward Peregrine. The other one, the one who now had a broken arm, was on his feet again. He was so pale he looked like he was about to faint, but that wasn't going to be enough to stop him from attacking again.

Jarvis placed himself in front of Peregrine and growled. No matter how scared he was, he wasn't going to allow anyone to hurt Peregrine. He'd rather die.

The man moved, and Jarvis jumped. He pressed one of his paws against the arm he'd broken, causing the man to scream again. This time, Jarvis didn't hesitate. He clamped his mouth around the man's throat and tore it out, closing his eyes as he did so. He felt it when the life went out of the man, and they both dropped onto the floor.

Jarvis didn't take the time to think about what he'd done. He spat out the blood and flesh in his mouth and turned toward the broken ankle guy. Thankfully, that one was dragging himself to the door. He didn't even look back at the man Jarvis had killed.

Jarvis watched him disappear into the hallway, but he didn't move, even though he and Peregrine were alone now — well, alone with a dead body. Adrenaline coursed through him, and he knew that if someone else attacked, he would be able to defend Peregrine.

He jerked when a hand touched the back of his neck. He twisted around, but it was only Peregrine who stood there with his hands raised.

"I'm not going to hurt you," he promised.

Jarvis shifted. He slammed the door shut, even though he suspected he and Peregrine wouldn't be able to stay here much longer. Someone was bound to have heard what had happened.

Jarvis looked down at himself. He needed another shower since he was dirty with blood, and he felt like he was about to throw up. "I know you're not," he croaked.

He wondered if Peregrine was scared of him, but before he

could ask, Peregrine moved toward him. He cupped one of Jarvis's cheeks with his hand and looked him in the eyes. "I think we should call Cam," he said.

Jarvis chuckled, but it sounded more like a sob. "I think we should," he agreed.

"You saved me. They would have taken me away, but you didn't hesitate. Thank you." He didn't say that Jarvis had killed for him, even though he had.

"I'd do anything for you. I thought you knew that by now."

Peregrine smiled. "Maybe I should have."

He hesitated, then, stunning Jarvis, he leaned forward and kissed him on the lips.

Jarvis couldn't react for a few seconds. Once he could, he was torn between kissing Peregrine back and pushing him away because his mouth tasted of blood. In the end, he decided to kiss Peregrine back for a few moments so he wouldn't think Jarvis didn't want this.

Peregrine leaned back, smiling but wrinkling his nose. "That wasn't the way I thought our first kiss would happen," he murmured.

"Too much blood?" Jarvis asked.

Peregrine nodded, then stepped away and looked around. "You should shower again and brush your teeth. We need to be out of here as soon as possible before someone comes to see what happened."

Jarvis sighed. Hopefully, this hadn't been their first and last kiss. He wouldn't find out now, so he turned toward the bathroom to obey. The sooner they went home, the better it would be.

CHAPTER FIVE

Peregrine looked around the forest just in case someone was there. The only people around were part of the pack, though, and he forced himself to relax. It wasn't easy, and for the few days he and Jarvis had been back in Rosewood, he'd been jumpy and hypervigilant.

That wasn't going to change anytime soon. He was terrified someone would find and hurt them, and he never wanted that to happen.

He did enjoy being with Jarvis, though. They hadn't kissed again since that day in the motel, and they hadn't talked about being mates. He didn't know if they would. Jarvis had been through a lot. He'd killed for Peregrine, and Peregrine didn't know how to deal with that. He could only imagine how Jarvis felt about it. They hadn't talked, but maybe they should.

Things were awkward between them in a way they'd never been. Jarvis was hesitant and shy, more so than before, but he was also gentle and caring, and he didn't seem to blame Peregrine for what had happened.

Peregrine wouldn't have blamed him if he had. He felt responsible. He should have pushed Jarvis to go back home instead of agreeing he could stay. He should have run while Jarvis was in the shower, but he'd promised he wouldn't, and he hadn't wanted to break a second promise. It was his fault Jarvis had attacked those two guys, and it was his fault Jarvis had needed to kill one of them.

"You're doing it again," Jarvis said.

He leaned against the tree they'd chosen to have their

picnic under. It was all very cute and sappy, and it made Peregrine feel like nothing had happened. He could almost forget about the few days he and Jarvis had spent on the run, which was a problem.

He still didn't know whether or not he should stay. Cam and Toby hadn't been angry or even disappointed. They'd both been understanding, but they'd also told Peregrine that no matter what happened, Rosewood was his home. If he wanted to stay, they would do everything they could to defend him, which meant putting themselves and the pack in danger. Peregrine had already put Jarvis in danger as it was. He didn't think he could deal with putting the entire pack at risk.

"Peregrine?" Jarvis sounded worried now.

Peregrine shook himself and smiled at him. "Sorry. I was lost in my thoughts."

Jarvis stared at him for a moment before nodding. "I know. It was kind of obvious. Are you okay?"

Peregrine didn't know how to answer that. "I have no idea," he said honestly.

Jarvis reached for his hand but stopped before taking it. He started to retreat, but Peregrine had enough of this. He reached out, taking Jarvis's hand in his and squeezing. Then he settled against the trunk of the tree next to Jarvis, with their shoulders pressed together.

"I'm not sure how I feel, either," Jarvis said.

"What about your parents? You never told me what they said when you came back."

Even though Jarvis was back in pack territory, he'd moved out of his parents' house. Peregrine had never met them, and Jarvis hadn't talked about what had happened, but Toby had. He'd been disappointed with Jarvis's mother, who had refused to allow him to move out, even though he was twenty-six. She was acting like he was still a child, which made

Peregrine angry. Thankfully, Jarvis hadn't given in, and he was staying in the room next to Peregrine's.

Peregrine kind of wished he were staying in *his* room.

But he didn't know how Jarvis felt about him. They'd kissed after Jarvis had killed that man, but they'd both been freaking out and full of adrenaline. Were things different now? Jarvis seemed to have taken a step back, but that could be because of how he was. He'd always been hesitant, even when Peregrine had told him he wanted them to be friends or when they'd realized they were mates. Maybe the same was happening now.

Jarvis sighed. "I should talk about that, shouldn't I?"

"Not if you don't want to. But Toby mentioned something about your mother, and I wanted you to know that I'm here if you need anything."

Jarvis leaned harder against Peregrine's shoulder. Peregrine took a risk and raised his arm, wrapping it around Jarvis's shoulders. Jarvis squeaked, but he didn't move, and Peregrine pulled him closer.

"She's not taking this well. I have to see her once we're done here."

"She didn't want you to move out."

"I can't say I don't understand why. I left home through the window without telling her or anyone else what was going on. She woke up, and my bedroom was empty. She thought I was dead, and once I came back, I guess she didn't want me to be out of her sight. I just don't get it. She never cared much about me. Why does she now?"

"I think she always cared about you," Peregrine said slowly. He didn't want to say the wrong thing, but he also didn't want Jarvis to lose his parents because of him, no matter how angry he was at them.

"Maybe. It's not like they neglected me or anything like that, but we're not close. Why is she freaking out that way?

Besides, I'm twenty-six. Didn't she know she couldn't forbid me to go?"

"I think she was still scared and tried to keep you close."

"Yeah, well, I couldn't stay. Being with you made me realize it's time for me to make a change. I've been complaining a lot about how they treat me, but I've allowed it to continue." His cheeks flushed. "Not that we're together that way."

Peregrine blinked. "What do you mean?"

"I said being with you, but I meant when we were on the run, not us being a couple because we obviously aren't, even with, well, everything."

Was this what had happened? Peregrine should have realized. He'd kissed Jarvis, hoping it was enough to tell Jarvis how he felt about him. Maybe Jarvis thought it was an accident or that Peregrine had already forgotten about it. Peregrine had to be honest and open with him, in ways he'd never been with anyone else. Otherwise, they wouldn't understand each other, and something like this would happen again.

It was time to talk.

Peregrine straightened and slipped away from Jarvis. He turned around so he could face him and leaned closer. "Is that what you think?"

Jarvis frowned. "What do I think?"

"That we're not together? Why do you think I kissed you?"

Jarvis's eyes widened, and he looked away. "Honestly? I have no clue. I've been wondering about that since you did, but I didn't want to ask. I thought that maybe it was a spur of the moment thing."

It was, but that didn't mean Peregrine regretted it. "I kissed you because I like you." He more than liked Jarvis, but that felt too fragile, and it was too soon to tell him. "And we're mates."

Peregrine didn't know what would happen between them or with the people who were after him. He might have to leave the pack after all, and if he did, he wasn't taking Jarvis with him. He couldn't allow Jarvis to ruin his life any more than he already had. Jarvis had done so much for him. He'd made Peregrine feel safe and like he wasn't alone in the world, and he'd killed a man. He shouldn't have had to, but he had, and Peregrine wanted to make sure he never had to do anything like that ever again.

"Well, yeah, I know you like me. We wouldn't be friends otherwise."

Peregrine shook his head. "Not like that. I like you as a guy. As a boyfriend, I guess. As a mate, although that feels like a lot right now."

Jarvis stared.

Peregrine didn't understand how he hadn't expected this, but then, he wasn't Jarvis.

Gosh. He was going to strangle Jarvis's parents if he ever met them. They might not have meant to, but they'd made him feel like he wasn't enough, and now, Jarvis couldn't shake that idea.

Peregrine leaned forward and cupped both of Jarvis's cheeks. He kissed the tip of his nose, then, when Jarvis didn't move away, his lips. The kiss was short and gentle, and Jarvis's eyes were still wide when Peregrine leaned back. "I know the situation is far from ideal, but I want to be with you. I can't make any promises. I told Cam and Toby I'd stay, and I will, but not if it means putting you and the pack in danger. But for as long as I'm here, if you want me, I'm yours."

To Peregrine's surprise, Jarvis surged forward and kissed him. This time it wasn't short. Jarvis wrapped his arms around Peregrine and pulled him against his body, and Peregrine fell against him. He ended up straddling Jarvis's thighs, his hands buried in Jarvis's hair as they kissed.

Peregrine didn't know what the future held, but for once, he knew that if he could, he would stay.

Jarvis had no idea what was happening, but he wasn't about to protest. Having Peregrine in his arms was overwhelming in the best of ways. He wished he could stay here for the rest of the afternoon because it had been perfect.

He couldn't remember who'd had the idea of having a picnic. It was probably Peregrine, since Jarvis would never have thought about anything like that. But who it was didn't matter, not when the afternoon had been so perfect.

Jarvis had put together a basket with food and drinks, and they'd found an isolated place that wasn't so deep in the forest that they couldn't get help if they needed it. They'd sat under a tree, eating and drinking, and in the beginning, not talking much. Jarvis honestly had thought they were back to being just friends, and it had been fine with him.

But they were more. Peregrine was *so* much more than a friend, and Jarvis still couldn't believe he was in his arms — or that they were kissing.

He didn't know how long they stayed like that. Eventually, Peregrine's hands started to roam over what he could reach of Jarvis's body, and even though it made Jarvis uncomfortable, he didn't try to stop him. He knew Peregrine would stop if he as much as said a word about it, but he wanted this, and Peregrine would never say anything about the way he looked. He seemed to enjoy Jarvis's body, and while Jarvis didn't understand why, he didn't think it mattered.

So he did some exploring of his own. Peregrine was slim and strong but also pliant under Jarvis's hands. He made a sound like a purr when Jarvis scratched his back, even though it was through his shirt. Jarvis promised himself to do it again, hopefully with Peregrine's shirt off. He wished he could do it now, but he'd promised his mother he would visit her, and he wanted to make sure she didn't freak out like she had when he'd gone after Peregrine.

The next time Peregrine kissed down Jarvis's neck, Jarvis put his hands on his shoulders and gently pushed. Peregrine blinked as if he couldn't remember what was happening outside their bubble.

"What?" he asked.

"I have to go see my mother." And maybe it was time to tell her who Peregrine was to him. Jarvis and Peregrine still hadn't talked about what being mates meant to them, but they'd acknowledged that they were. Jarvis supposed everything else could wait. He wasn't in a rush to be anything but Peregrine's boyfriend. Being mates felt too big and important, especially with Peregrine still poised to run.

Peregrine sighed. "I understand." He hesitated. "I'll see you later, then?"

Jarvis was pretty sure he would regret it, but he still said, "You can come with me."

"I've never met anyone's parents. Well, I've never had a boyfriend, so I guess *everything* is new right now."

"And I've never had anyone meet my parents, not as my boyfriend." And he still couldn't believe he and Peregrine were boyfriends.

They could have been since that kiss at the motel, but Jarvis had been too much of a coward to ask Peregrine why he'd done it and how he felt now that they were back home. He'd lost a few days with Peregrine, but maybe he hadn't. They'd always been friends, and now, they were friends who kissed.

He couldn't wait to see what else they would do together.

"You don't have to come if you don't want to. It's probably going to be awkward and awful, but I promised her I would go, and I can't go back on that promise. She freaked out when I left, and I feel guilty about that."

Peregrine climbed off Jarvis's legs. "As you should. You ran away from home."

Jarvis glared. "I didn't run away. I'm twenty-six, for fuck's sake."

Peregrine smiled. "All right. You still could have left her a note or something."

"Maybe." Jarvis *should* have left her a note, but he doubted it would have changed anything.

To him, it felt like his mother was more freaked out about losing control over him than because he'd gone with Peregrine. He'd refused to tell her what happened while they were away, and he'd made Cam and Toby promise they wouldn't, either. With the number of people who'd come to pick up him and Peregrine from the motel, though, he suspected that eventually, someone would talk. But he didn't live with her anymore, and he wasn't planning on ever moving back. Cam and Toby had told him he could stay with them as long as he wanted, and even though things had been awkward in the beginning, Jarvis loved it. They didn't treat him like a child or like he was easily dismissible. They treated him like a person, and at the same time, like someone they cared about.

Peregrine got to his feet and offered Jarvis his hand. Jarvis only hesitated for a moment before taking it and allowing Peregrine to pull him to his feet. They didn't talk as they packed things up, but they kept peeking at each other, and by the time they were done, Jarvis was beaming. His heart felt like it was about to explode when Peregrine took his hand, and they started walking toward Jarvis's parents' house.

Jarvis had no idea how his mother would react, but right now, he didn't care.

She was watching out the window when they arrived. That was the only explanation for why she threw open the door before he could even climb up the porch steps. She stared at them, her eyes wide, then turned her attention to Jarvis. "What's going on?" she asked.

Jarvis's mouth was dry, but he pushed ahead. "Mom, this

is Peregrine, my boyfriend. Peregrine, this is my mom, Angela."

"Is this the boy who took you away?"

Jarvis sighed. "For one, he's not a boy. He's almost thirty. And no, he didn't take me away. I went with him because I wanted to protect him, and I did."

"He put you in danger. It's a miracle nothing happened to you, and I can't believe you'd still want to be with him."

Jarvis wanted to tell her he'd put himself in danger on his own, but he couldn't.

"I'm sorry, Peregrine, but you're not welcome here," she continued. "And Jarvis, you need to move your things back. I don't believe you should be living on your own, but especially not with this man."

Jarvis swallowed. He couldn't allow this to happen, and while facing his mother was even more terrifying than facing those two guys in the motel, he couldn't do what she wanted.

"This isn't the right way to show him you love him," Peregrine said.

He sounded calm, but his hand was tight around Jarvis's.

Jarvis's mother sucked in a breath. "I'm sorry?"

Peregrine stood taller. "You should be. When I met Jarvis, he thought so little of himself that he couldn't believe I wanted to be his friend. He thinks he's boring and not good enough, and you're the reason he believes that. I don't know anything about you, and I don't want to judge you, but you're doing it again. You're treating him like he can't make his own decisions, even though he's twenty-six. I don't understand if it's because you're worried about him or because you're losing control, and honestly, I don't care. I don't think it matters, either. If you want what's best for your son, you need to allow him to do what he wants, and more importantly, you need to look at your behavior and correct it. Jarvis has to understand what a wonderful person he is. He has to realize he's not boring and that he's more than good enough. He is for me. Can you say the same?"

Jarvis gaped. He couldn't believe Peregrine had stood up to his mother that way, although maybe he should. Peregrine had never been shy when it came to saying what he thought.

"I don't—what are you talking about?" Jarvis's mom asked. "Jarvis?"

Jarvis looked her in the eyes. "He's right. You always made me feel like I wasn't as good as Melissa, Todd, and Kyle. I don't know why. Maybe it's because I look ordinary next to them. Maybe it's because I've never been popular in school or good at sports like they were. But treating me that way meant that *they* treated me the same way, and it hurt."

It still did. That was why Jarvis didn't have a good relationship with any of his siblings, even though he loved them. It hadn't been easy, not when their mother favored them.

But Jarvis wasn't alone anymore. He had Peregrine by his side, standing up for him, and it helped him stand up for himself, too. He didn't know if he would have had the courage to do it if he were still on his own, but he wasn't. If he had it his way, he would never be on his own again because Peregrine would stay in Rosewood with him.

Peregrine wasn't sure what had pushed him to tell Jarvis's mother all of that, but he didn't regret it. The only way he would was if Jarvis yelled at him for being rude. But it had to be done, and Peregrine wasn't sure Jarvis would have done it if it hadn't been for him.

Jarvis cared about his parents, and Peregrine hoped his parents cared about him. Love wasn't always enough, though, and in this case, it hadn't been. Jarvis's mother at least had favored her other children over him. It meant she'd never gotten to know her son and that she'd never found out how wonderful he was. She never would if she didn't stop doing this.

"I didn't know you felt that way," she murmured. "I didn't know I did that."

"But you did," Jarvis told her. "And now that you know, you can try changing things. I'm not saying you weren't a good mother, because you were, but mostly when it comes to feeding me and keeping a roof over my head. Emotionally, I was a mess, and I still am. I'm sorry all of this had to happen for me to tell you or even to realize it. But you need to let me live my life. I'm more than able to do it, even though you don't seem to believe it." He paused. "And by the way, Peregrine isn't just my boyfriend. He's my mate, and I'm never leaving him."

She was still staring, but Jarvis turned around, pulling Peregrine along with him. Peregrine followed. He would have followed him anywhere. He was stunned that Jarvis had admitted they were mates, but it didn't scare him as much as it had initially. They had many things to figure out, but them being mates meant something, even though Peregrine wasn't a hundred percent sure what.

"I can't believe I did that," Jarvis whispered as soon as they were far enough away that she wouldn't hear them.

Peregrine stopped walking and turned them so they could look at each other. "I'm proud of you."

Jarvis shook his head. "I barely did anything. *You* were the one who stood up to her. I should have done it, but instead, I needed you to do it for me."

"And that's fine. We're together, aren't we?" Peregrine needed Jarvis to understand that.

Jarvis nodded, and Peregrine sighed in relief.

"Then it's normal for me to stand up for you," he continued. "You're my boyfriend. My *mate*. I want you to be happy, and if standing up to your mother makes that happen, I'll do it again and again. She should never have treated you the way she did, and I hope she realizes that now. But if she doesn't, if she continues insisting that she should control your life instead of allowing you to do what you need and want to do, I'll do it again."

Peregrine wanted to kiss Jarvis, and since they were together, he could. He cupped Jarvis's face and kissed him, not caring that Jarvis's mother might see them or that they were in the middle of the forest. He didn't care who saw them. He wasn't afraid of being with Jarvis, and one day, Jarvis would understand that.

Unfortunately, the kiss was interrupted by Peregrine's phone vibrating in his pocket. He wanted to ignore it, but he'd learned a long time ago that he couldn't afford to ignore anyone who called him. Very few people had his number, and they only called when it was important.

He gave Jarvis one last kiss, then stepped away. He took his phone out of his pocket, looked at the screen, and answered. "Yes?"

"Peregrine?"

"It's me.

"You're the caladrius shifter?"

"I am."

"My name is Everly. I'm part of the rare shifters network."

Peregrine's stomach felt like it turned to lead. There could only be one reason for them to call. Well, maybe more, but both would involve him leaving Rosewood, and he wasn't ready to do that a second time. Still, he couldn't hang up. "I'm listening."

"I'm sorry to say this, but we have news that someone is in Rosewood trying to find you."

Peregrine blinked. "How do you know I'm in Rosewood?"

He could almost hear the smile in Everly's voice when he answered. "You didn't think we would abandon you, did you? Ever since Alpha Smith, the dire wolf alpha, found out about you, he's been keeping an eye on you just in case something happens. He can't do much since he doesn't live in Rosewood, but he's kept in contact with us and asked us to keep you safe, too. That's why when we heard that people are in Rosewood, we knew we had to contact you."

Peregrine reached for the closest tree. He pressed his palm against the bark, needing the rough feeling to keep him from freaking out.

His first instinct was to run, but he couldn't. He'd promised Jarvis he would never do that again, and he had every intention of keeping that promise.

"Do you have more information?"

"Unfortunately, not much. You know how our network works. We rely on hearsay and people calling these things in, and it's never precise. What I do know is that the people after you answer to a woman called Leanna."

Peregrine had never heard that name, but he wasn't surprised. Many more people than what he knew of were after him. Once they found out what he could do, they always did everything they could to get their hands on him. "Thanks for telling me."

"Don't worry about it, and let me know if you need anything else. We might not be good when it comes to protection, but if there's anything we can do, we'll help."

"I don't know how to thank you."

"You don't have to. You'd to do the same for any of us. We're rare shifters, and most of us are hunted. We're a family, and we need to act like it. I'll send all information I have to your number."

Peregrine was dazed when they hung up. He looked at Jarvis, who was staring at him. "They're coming," he said.

Jarvis continued staring for a while before nodding. "I'm surprised you're not running."

Peregrine chuckled darkly. "I won't deny that was my first instinct, but I won't break another promise to you. I'm not going anywhere, not until you decide you don't want me anymore."

Jarvis snorted. "That's never going to happen." He moved closer and took Peregrine's hand. "Come on. We need to get to Cam."

They ran through the forest. Peregrine couldn't help but look around, wondering if they'd already found him and if they were watching him even now. That wasn't the case, but it certainly felt like it.

When they got to Cam's house, Peregrine looked at Jarvis. "You should go home. I know you want to be here for me, and I'm grateful, but I don't want you to put yourself in any more danger than you've already been."

Jarvis shook his head. "I'm not going anywhere. You and I are together. That means we do this together."

Peregrine wouldn't get Jarvis to change his mind, so he didn't ask again. Instead, they walked in and went straight to Cam's office. They found him with Toby. Both of them looked up when Jarvis knocked on the open door of Cam's office.

Toby started to smile, but Cam looked grim. "You don't have good news," he said.

He didn't look surprised.

"I just got a phone call from someone who's part of the rare shifter network. Someone is looking for me in Rosewood."

Cam nodded. "I'm not surprised. Someone has been in town asking for you, and they even reached pack territory."

Peregrine needed to sit down. He grabbed the closest chair and dropped into it. "What happened?"

"The twins sent them away, and they didn't linger or protest. I'm not sure if it's because they weren't ready to do anything else or because they recognized the twins as phoenix shifters, but it doesn't matter. It's a problem, and we have to deal with it." Cam took a deep breath. "I can't promise you nothing will happen, but I and everyone else in the pack will do everything we can to keep you safe. We need you to stay with us to be able to do that, though."

"I already promised I wouldn't run again." Peregrine's voice was rough, and his eyes burned.

"And I hope you'll keep that promise. You're a pack member, Peregrine. You're not fighting alone anymore, and I want you to remember that."

Jarvis couldn't stop peeking at Peregrine. He understood how worried Peregrine was, and he wasn't the only one. Jarvis wished he could take Peregrine and run away with him, but it didn't work well for them, as the past experience had shown. That meant they had to stay in Rosewood, where they were safe and surrounded by people who knew how to fight. Jarvis wasn't looking forward to possibly having to kill someone again.

He had nightmares about the man he'd killed. Logically, he knew there hadn't been another way to help Peregrine. Even though both of the men who'd attacked them had been wounded, Jarvis doubted they would have stopped until they got what they wanted. He'd been lucky he'd managed to get to that guy's throat, because if he hadn't, he would have been killed and Peregrine would have disappeared. No one would have known what had happened, and it would have been Jarvis's fault.

Knowing that didn't help. He couldn't stop thinking about the man he'd killed and wonder if he'd had a family, maybe a wife and children. Did they know he was dead? Or were they worried about him, wondering what had happened to him? Jarvis didn't even know if the police had intervened, but he'd looked for it on the Internet, and apparently, no one had found a body. That meant that whoever had sent those people had intervened, and that they were much more powerful than Jarvis had expected. If they could make a body disappear without anyone wondering what had happened, they wouldn't hesitate to do whatever they needed to get to Peregrine.

"All right," Peregrine said.

"Are you agreeing to be a pack member?" Cam asked.

"I don't seem to have a choice. You guys already decided I was part of the pack."

"You don't have to be if you don't want to. You don't even have to stay, although I hope you will, at least until you're safe."

Peregrine snorted. "I'll never be safe, and I don't want to leave. I also don't want to bring trouble to your door, though. That's why I left, and I would have stayed away if Jarvis hadn't intervened."

Jarvis's cheeks flushed, but he wasn't ashamed of going after Peregrine. He would do it again if he had to, and he also would kill again if it meant saving his boyfriend.

That was going to take some time to get used to.

"As long as you trust us to keep you safe, we'll deal with everything else once the danger is over," Cam said. "I think you should move out of our house."

Peregrine's eyes widened. "I thought you wanted me to stay."

He was freaking out, and Jarvis didn't blame him. He trusted Cam, though, so he knew something was coming.

"We do want you to stay," Cam agreed. "And if one day, you decide you want your own house, we'll be more than happy to accommodate that. In the meantime, while these people are still in town asking questions about you, I think it would be safer if you and Jarvis, if he wants to go with you, disappeared for a bit."

"Where would we go? They found us at that motel. They won't have a problem finding us at another."

Cam shook his head. "You won't be going to a motel."

"You'll go to my childhood home," Toby intervened.

Both Jarvis and Peregrine turned to look at him. Jarvis knew what he was talking about, even though he'd never seen the place. As far as he knew, it was a mess, although the pack had been working for a bit to fix it and make it habitable. He hadn't realized they'd managed or that they were going to use it as a safe house. He hadn't even realized the pack needed a safe house until recently, but with the recent influx of rare shifters, it didn't sound like a bad idea.

"I'm listening," Peregrine said.

"My brother and I used to live with our parents in the forest. The house is isolated, which they did on purpose because they didn't want people to find us. No one will know you're there. We won't even tell most pack members. It'll be on a need-to-know basis, and as far as I'm concerned, only the people in this room need to know where you are, along with the twins and the beta."

Peregrine slowly nodded. "You think no one will notice we're there?"

"It would be impossible. You won't have neighbors. We'll take care of security, and we'll bring food and anything else you might need. We don't know how long you'll have to stay there, but it's not uncomfortable, even though you'll be alone most of the time."

"I don't mind being alone," Peregrine said.

"I don't mind either," Jarvis added. He'd been alone most of his life, or at least, it felt like it. He thought it wouldn't be a bad idea for him to stay away from his mother for a while anyway. Now that he'd told her how he felt about the way she'd behaved, he thought she could do with some time to think about it. He was also afraid to find out how she would react, which made running away an appealing opportunity.

Cam got up from his chair. "All right. We'll move both of you now. You should go pack your things and be ready to leave in half an hour. It's a bit of a trek to get there, but nothing awful."

"You're coming with us?" Jarvis asked.

Cam shook his head. "I wish I could, but I don't want to risk leaving, just in case those people come back. Toby will walk you there, along with Lennox. They'll make sure you get there safe and sound. And of course, you'll have a cell phone to call us if you need anything. Call one of us, and we'll do what we can to accommodate you." He turned his attention to Jarvis. "You should visit your family. Don't tell them where you'll be staying but make it obvious that they won't be allowed to visit you. If things go well, you'll be able to visit while going back to the safe house the rest of the time."

Jarvis shook his head. "That won't be a problem. I just fought with my mother, and I doubt my siblings will want to see me." It wasn't like they cared what happened to him. His father might, but with how things had gone with Jarvis's mom, he didn't want to risk telling his father anything in case he passed it along to her.

Cam grimaced. "Sorry about that. It was a long time coming, wasn't it?"

"It was, and I should have stood up to her a long time ago. I hope that being away from the pack for a while will help."

"I know it will."

Peregrine and Jarvis separated to go to their bedrooms to pack. Jarvis had only moved into Cam's house a few days ago, but his backpack seemed to have exploded all over the room. It took him much longer than Peregrine to get everything together, and even then he had to leave some of the stuff behind. He hadn't realized he had so much accumulated, especially next to what belonged to Peregrine.

"I've been on the run my entire life," Peregrine said when he noticed Jarvis staring at his small backpack. "I never allowed myself to have much because I've been forced to abandon my things time and time again. It's not a bad thing that you own a lot of stuff."

Jarvis shrugged. "Maybe now that you're staying, you'll be able to buy the things you've always wanted."

The idea seemed to surprise Peregrine, but he nodded. "Maybe."

Toby and Lennox were waiting for them in the entrance. Cam was there, too, and patted their shoulders as they passed by him. "You'll be fine. We'll let you know if anything happens. In the meantime, stick to the safe house and contact no one but us. If you have anything urgent to deal with, let us know, and we'll do everything we can."

"My job," Jarvis said. He hadn't gone back to work yet because Cam had wanted to keep an eye on him, and now, it made sense. Still, he didn't have vacation days piled up.

"I'll talk to your boss," Cam promised. "And if anything goes wrong, I'll make sure you have another job once this is over."

Jarvis didn't want to lose his job at the coffee shop because he enjoyed it, but he had to choose, and he was choosing Peregrine.

They filed out of the house. A few weeks ago, all of this would have freaked Jarvis out, but today, he stuck close to Peregrine, holding his hand as they walked. They were silent, listening to Toby talk and Lennox grunt in answer. Jarvis was nervous, but he trusted Lennox to keep them safe. He was a phoenix shifter, and he could set fire to anyone or anything.

Jarvis didn't know how long they walked, but his feet started aching. He didn't say anything about it, not wanting to look weak, but he did suck in a breath when they suddenly walked into a clearing and a house stood in front of them.

Part of the house had collapsed, but part of it seemed to be fit for living. He hoped the collapsed part wouldn't be dangerous, but he doubted Cam would want them to stay here if it was.

Toby stopped by the front door and turned to them. "There's already food inside. We suspected something like this would happen, so we made sure it was stocked. There's not much, so I'll come back tomorrow with more food. You should be fine for the rest of today, though."

"Thank you," Peregrine said.

He looked overwhelmed, and Jarvis was, too.

"Stay safe, both of you. I'll see you tomorrow."

He didn't go inside the house, and neither did Lennox. Lennox tilted his head at Peregrine and Jarvis, then followed Toby back into the forest, leaving them alone with the house.

Jarvis swallowed and squeezed Peregrine's hand. "Ready to go in?" he asked.

"As ready as I ever will be."

CHAPTER SIX

There was only one bed.

Peregrine had thought it meant he and Jarvis would finally get beyond kissing, but so far, they hadn't. Not that he didn't enjoy kissing Jarvis. He did, very much so. But they'd been stuck together in the safe house for a few weeks already, and spending so much time with him made Peregrine want more. If it had been anyone but Jarvis, Peregrine would already have made a move. He was afraid of scaring Jarvis into running, though. He knew Jarvis still had doubts about how Peregrine felt about him, and he understood. Not even his parents saw him for the man he was.

But Jarvis and Peregrine had been through a lot together, and it had pushed them closer than Peregrine had ever been to anyone else. That had to mean something, and it did. Peregrine doubted he'd have been in love with Jarvis if they hadn't lived through all of that.

But since Jarvis was Jarvis and Peregrine loved him, he'd kept his distance, even when they were in bed—especially when they were in bed. He didn't want Jarvis to do anything he wasn't ready for or didn't want. But how would he know what Jarvis wanted? Jarvis always got flustered when Peregrine tried talking to him about it, and while it was adorable, it didn't help them move forward as a couple.

Maybe they didn't have to. Everything else was up in the air, after all. Jarvis couldn't go to work. He'd left his parents' house and hadn't seen them since he and Peregrine had moved to the safe house. Whoever was after Peregrine hadn't changed their minds, and even if they did, someone else would come in their place. It always happened, and Peregrine didn't think he'd ever be free.

But for the first time, he was safe, and he wasn't alone. Maybe things weren't that bad after all.

Sighing, he rolled to his side to look at Jarvis. Today wasn't the day they'd have sex, either, and that was fine with Peregrine. He had so much more than he'd ever thought he would, and he couldn't complain.

Jarvis was still sleeping. It was corny, but he looked at peace when he slept, and since they didn't have anything to do until later, Peregrine decided to let him sleep. They were going to a pack cookout this evening, even though Peregrine was worried. Cam himself had called him to reassure him and to tell him he didn't have to come if he didn't want to, but Peregrine did, and, more importantly, Jarvis did. Peregrine wasn't letting him out of his sight for now, which meant he would go to the cookout, too.

But that was tonight. For now, he got out of bed and headed to the bathroom. His dick was hard, and he didn't want Jarvis to be uncomfortable if he woke up. Peregrine was used to taking care of these situations on his own anyway. Most days, he ignored it, although it had become harder since he and Jarvis had started sharing a bed.

He didn't lock the door—there wasn't a need to—and he turned the shower on. Hopefully, Jarvis would sleep long enough that he wouldn't understand what Peregrine was up to.

Peregrine stripped, dropping his clothes to the floor. He reached for the shower curtain, but before he could push it aside, the door opened. He turned and stared at Jarvis, who stood there, looking barely awake but staring back. His hair was sticking up on one side of his head and his eyes were bleary, but that cleared up after he looked up and down

Peregrine's body and realized Peregrine was naked.

Jarvis squeaked and turned around, but he still didn't leave the bathroom. "Sorry!" he yelled.

Peregrine didn't try to hide his body. He wasn't ashamed of it, and he wanted to know if Jarvis liked it. He suspected that was the case. "It's not a problem. Do you need the bathroom before I shower?"

"I—maybe?"

Peregrine almost laughed. "Maybe?"

"I'm not sure anymore."

"I'm just going to go back to the bedroom, okay? Then you can do whatever you need to do."

To do that, Peregrine had to walk past Jarvis. He did so without touching him, and he didn't miss the way Jarvis's gaze followed him. Jarvis squeaked again, and Peregrine was ready to bet he was blushing.

The bathroom door slammed shut. Peregrine leaned against the wall by it with his arms crossed over his chest. It took about five minutes for Jarvis to come out, and by the time he did, Peregrine had worked himself up imagining how differently the situation could have gone. What if Jarvis had offered to join him in the bathroom? He'd look so good wearing only water and soap, and Peregrine would almost imagine dragging his hands all over his body.

There was no way for him to hide his erection when the door opened again. He didn't try because, once again, he wasn't ashamed.

Jarvis was trying hard not to look down at Peregrine's groin. "Sorry about that, and thank you."

"What for?"

"Letting me use the bathroom. You can shower now if you want. Well, I'm sure you do. You were about to when I barged in. Anyway, I'll just go get breakfast ready if that's okay with you?"

Jarvis moved toward the bedroom door without waiting for an answer, but Peregrine wasn't done. He caught Jarvis's wrist and pulled him close, and Jarvis being Jarvis, he managed to trip on his own feet. Peregrine caught him and held him close, inhaling the scent he could now recognize even with his eyes shut. Jarvis smelled of honey and something flowery, and to Peregrine, that was the best scent in the world.

"Peregrine?" Jarvis whispered.

Peregrine kissed him. He hoped Jarvis would understand what he was trying to say because he wasn't sure he could find the words to explain just how important Jarvis was to him.

Thankfully, Jarvis leaned against Peregrine instead of pushing him away. He wrapped his arms around Peregrine and kissed him back hungrily. Peregrine hoped he was about to get what he so desperately wanted and started walking Jarvis backward toward the bed. He felt the hesitancy in the way Jarvis moved, but Jarvis didn't protest, not even when they reached the bed and Peregrine lowered both of them to the mattress.

When Peregrine leaned back to look at Jarvis, he thought Jarvis had never looked so beautiful, and since Jarvis needed to hear that, he said it out loud. "You're gorgeous."

Jarvis's cheeks blazed, and he looked away. "I'm not."

"Well, I think you are, and I hope that eventually, you'll believe me when I say it." Peregrine licked his lips and glided a hand toward the bottom of Jarvis's t-shirt. "Can I take this off you?"

Jarvis audibly swallowed. "Do you have to?"

"No, but I'd like to feel your skin against mine. I don't have to look if you'd rather I don't." Peregrine wanted to, but he was patient and ready to give Jarvis the time he needed to get used to the idea he truly liked what he was seeing.

Jarvis still didn't look convinced, but he nodded. "Okay."

Peregrine made sure to keep his gaze on Jarvis's face as he tugged the t-shirt off him. Then he reached for Jarvis's pajama pants. He didn't have to ask, because Jarvis raised his hips to allow him to slide the pants down. He was still wearing underwear, and Peregrine hovered his hand above them, silently asking if he could take them off, too. Jarvis was as hard as he was, and while he had no idea what they were about to do, he didn't care. He just wanted Jarvis close and happy.

Jarvis licked his lips and nodded.

Peregrine kissed him as he pulled the underwear down. Jarvis was shaking just a bit, and Peregrine knew why. He was afraid Peregrine wouldn't like his body, and while Peregrine wished Jarvis believed him if he promised he did, he knew that wouldn't be the case. Jarvis would understand it in time, and that was okay. Peregrine would show him how much he loved everything about it time and time again.

He'd promised Jarvis he wouldn't look at his body, and he didn't, even though he wanted to. Instead, he continued kissing Jarvis as he touched him slowly. It meant he couldn't touch all of Jarvis's body, but that was okay, too. He stroked his skin until he got to the place where their cocks rubbed against each other. It felt so good already that Peregrine knew he wouldn't last, and he didn't want to. Their first time would be perfect because it was them, no matter how long it lasted or what happened.

Feeling Jarvis's skin against his took the breath away from Peregrine. It was soft, and Peregrine couldn't wait to kiss every inch of it. Instead, he wrapped his fingers around both their cocks and pulled.

Jarvis whimpered and clung to Peregrine's shoulders. His mouth dropped open and their kisses changed, but that didn't make them any less incredible. Their cocks were slick with both their precum, for which Peregrine was grateful because it meant he didn't have to stop to grab the lube. He wasn't even sure there was any lube in the house. That was probably the one thing Toby hadn't thought to stock up on.

But they didn't need it. They kissed again and again, their tongues stroking at each other as Peregrine jacked them off. Jarvis came first, shivering in Peregrine's arms, digging his nail into Peregrine's shoulders in the sweetest pain he could ever feel.

He swallowed the sounds Jarvis made with his mouth, sucked on his tongue, and followed him down the pleasure lane. He screwed his eyes shut when he came, knowing they would do this time and time again and that this was just another step forward in their relationship. He didn't know what would happen next or how long he'd be on the run, but even if it was for the rest of his life, he wasn't alone anymore. He had Jarvis, and he was never letting him go.

He moved to his side, but he didn't let go of Jarvis. He continued kissing him as they both tried getting their breathing under control, and Jarvis kissed him back.

Then he swore. "We left the water on in the shower."

Peregrine rolled to his back and laughed. He loved Jarvis, and he was going to have to tell him that, but not until they weren't sticky anymore.

As they walked toward the cookout, Jarvis felt like he was floating. He hadn't been able to stop smiling since he and Peregrine had gotten up that morning, and he didn't think he would for the rest of the day.

It didn't make sense. He hadn't felt that way the other times he'd had sex with someone. But it was the first time he was in love with the man he was with, and Peregrine was special. He was so special that Jarvis hadn't thought they would end up doing this. No matter what Peregrine said, no matter the bond between them, Jarvis always expected him to leave once the danger was over. He still might, but Jarvis had decided not to think about that. Peregrine had promised he was staying, and as far as Jarvis was concerned, he would keep that promise.

Peregrine hadn't even gotten angry when Jarvis didn't want him to see his body. Jarvis knew it was stupid. He wasn't ugly, and the sex would have been so much better if he hadn't tried to hide. His body was ordinary, and it wasn't a reason for him to hide, especially not from Peregrine, who never said anything bad about him. Jarvis hadn't been able to help it, but he hoped that in time, he'd manage to be with Peregrine without fear and worry.

"Will your parents be there?" Peregrine asked.

Jarvis was so distracted that Peregrine's voice made him stumble on a tree root. He managed to catch himself against a tree trunk, and while he knew his cheeks were flushed, he didn't care. Peregrine seemed to find that adorable, and while it wasn't a word Jarvis associated with himself, he didn't mind if that was how Peregrine saw him.

"As far as I know," he answered.

Peregrine tried to hide it, but Jarvis didn't miss his grimace. "Do you think you'll want to talk to them?"

That was a hard question to answer. Jarvis wanted to see his parents and even his siblings to reassure them that he was okay, but he wasn't looking forward to fighting with any of them. "I won't avoid them if they try to talk to me, but I don't think I'll go out of my way to find them." Because it still hurt. Peregrine had always believed in Jarvis, something that still didn't make sense, even with their bond. Jarvis's parents should have done the same, and they hadn't. Jarvis was angry, and he needed some time away, which was one of the reasons he'd been so excited at the thought of spending time in the safe house alone with Peregrine.

The other reason was, well, spending time alone with

Peregrine.

Jarvis could hear music and voices now, which meant they were almost there. He looked down at Peregrine's hand, which was hanging by his side, and decided to take a risk. He doubted Peregrine would say no or pull away, not after what they'd shared that morning. Jarvis needed to have more faith in Peregrine — and himself.

He reached out and took Peregrine's hand.

Peregrine's eyes widened, but he smiled, and Jarvis knew he'd done the right thing. Together, they walked into the clearing where the pack houses stood.

Everyone was by the fire pit at the center of the loose arc their houses created. Cam and Reece were cooking meat on the fire, and the long tables close by were heavy with food. Everyone had contributed something, and it felt good to see the entire pack gathered. They didn't do this often because it was hard to find the right day for everyone to be there, and Jarvis wouldn't have missed this for anything in the world.

He couldn't help but smile. He never talked to most of the people gathered here, but it didn't matter. He was still part of the pack, and he belonged, no matter what he told himself.

He and Peregrine looked at each other, then they stepped forward and walked into the crowd. Jarvis noticed Sam and Toby standing by one of the tables, and they both waved at him when they saw him. He started pulling Peregrine toward them, but someone walked right into his path, forcing him to stop.

He looked at his brother. He was wary of talking to him or anyone from his family, but he couldn't avoid it. He wasn't even sure he wanted to.

He cleared his throat. "Peregrine, this is my brother, Kyle. Kyle, this is my boyfriend. My mate." Jarvis still wasn't used to that, and he wasn't sure he ever would be.

Kyle didn't look surprised, so obviously, their parents had

told him about Peregrine. Jarvis wasn't sure if that was a good thing. His mother wasn't happy with Peregrine's presence in his life.

But Kyle smiled. "It's a pleasure to meet you," he told Peregrine. He turned his attention back to Jarvis. "I'd like to talk to you if that's okay?"

Jarvis hesitated. "We just arrived. We should say hello."

"I promise I'll be fast."

"I'll go say hi to Toby and Sam," Peregrine murmured. He squeezed Jarvis's hand. "I'll be just there. You can join me as soon as you're done."

Jarvis nodded and let go of Peregrine's hand. He didn't want to, but he couldn't avoid his brother. Besides, it was better to talk to him than to his mother. Jarvis hadn't seen her yet, but he had no doubt she was in the crowd.

Kyle waited until Peregrine was gone to say, "I'm sorry."

Jarvis blinked, unsure what he was apologizing about. "What for?"

Kyle rubbed the back of his neck. "The way I behaved. The way I treated you. Hell, the way the *entire family* treated you. It wasn't right, and we should have realized sooner. I'm ashamed to say I might not have if I hadn't heard your boyfriend stand up for you against Mom."

Jarvis gaped. "You were there?"

Kyle nodded. "I wanted to come to you, but I knew Mom's head would explode if I tried to intervene. I thought I'd have time to talk to you later, but then you were whisked away, and I couldn't reach you. He's right, though. The family mistreated you, and it was horrible of us. I'm sorry."

Jarvis didn't know what to say. He hadn't expected that, and he still wasn't sure he'd heard Kyle right. Kyle had never been mean to Jarvis, but then, neither had Melissa and Todd. They had just never really noticed him. Melissa was ten years older, so it made sense, but Todd was only four years older, and Kyle two years younger. Jarvis had always watched people who were close to their siblings with envy, and he wondered if now, he would have that, too. He wasn't sure he wanted it, but also that he didn't.

"Thank you," he said. What else could he say after what Kyle had just explained?

Kyle looked disappointed, but he nodded. "I know you can't come home and that you probably don't want to, but I'm glad we talked and that you're okay. You're staying safe?"

For a wild moment, Jarvis thought he was talking about sex. But then he remembered that no one knew what had happened between him and Peregrine that morning and that his brother was talking about him being at the safe house. "I'm not the one in danger. I'm staying with Peregrine because he shouldn't be alone, but even if someone finds us, they won't come for me."

"That doesn't mean you're not in danger. If someone tries to get to Peregrine, they'll have to go through you, won't they?"

Jarvis couldn't deny that. He'd already put himself in front of Peregrine once, and he'd protected him. He would do it again if he had to, even if it meant killing another man. But his brother didn't know he'd killed someone, and he had no intention of telling him. He wasn't ready, and he also didn't want to see horror or disgust in Kyle's expression. Jarvis didn't know what Kyle would think of it or what would happen between them, but he didn't want to lose his brother.

Kyle patted Jarvis's shoulder. "You should go back to your mate. He's been glaring at me as if he's trying to dig a hole between my eyes with his gaze. I can't say I blame him, after what Mom said to him, but I hope that eventually we can become friends, or at the very least, friendly."

"I'm sure you will," Jarvis murmured. He had no way to know, but if he asked, Peregrine would do it, or at least, he'd *try* to be friends with Kyle.

Thankfully, Kyle didn't linger. He turned around and lost himself in the crowd, and Jarvis took a moment to wrap his mind around what had happened. Then he noticed his mother coming toward him, and he turned around and rushed toward where Peregrine was still standing. He knew he wouldn't be able to avoid her forever, but right now, the last thing he wanted was to talk to her.

Peregrine was relieved when Jarvis came back to him. He'd been happy but wary when Kyle had wanted to talk to his brother, and he'd hoped Jarvis wouldn't get hurt. It didn't seem like that was the case, even though Jarvis was now rushing toward him. Peregrine understood why when he saw Jarvis's mother behind him. She was still trying to get to him, but once he reached Peregrine, she stopped and glared.

Peregrine glared right back. He was still angry at how Jarvis's parents—his mother especially—had treated him. If Jarvis didn't want to talk to her, he shouldn't have to.

"You're protective of him," Toby said.

"Aren't you protective of Cam?"

Toby grinned. "That I am. It's just strange to see, since you were insisting you had to leave as soon as possible. You changed your mind."

Peregrine scowled. "I didn't change my mind as much as I realized I couldn't put Jarvis in that kind of danger." Because Jarvis would follow Peregrine anywhere he went, and Peregrine wouldn't force him to kill someone else, not even to defend him.

He'd already done that once, and it was more than enough. Jarvis should have a peaceful life, and he'd had it. Then, Peregrine had burst onto the scene, and he'd messed everything up. Jarvis didn't hold it against him, and he wasn't angry, but it didn't mean Peregrine wanted to risk him getting hurt.

Jarvis finally reached them, and Peregrine smiled at him. He offered Jarvis his hand, smiling when Jarvis took it without hesitation. He wasn't used to being open with his affections, but he wasn't trying to hide them, which was the important thing.

"She stopped coming after you," Peregrine murmured.

Jarvis leaned against him. "Thank God. I'm not ready to talk to her."

"And you don't have to."

"Eventually, I *will* have to, but it can wait. I already know what she's going to say anyway."

"You think she's still angry?"

"I know she is. She can't let things go. She never was able to. She hates that this isn't going the way she thinks it should go and that I'm not doing what she wants me to do anymore."

"She lost control."

Jarvis nodded. "And I never realized how much she cared about that." He turned toward Toby and Sam. "Hi. Sorry about all of this."

That put an end to the conversation about Jarvis's mother, but that was okay. Peregrine didn't want to talk about her. He wanted to forget about their problems and focus on having fun, eating too much food, and being together.

He'd never had this. Even when he'd allowed himself to spend time around people, he'd never been to a party. It was too exposed, and he hadn't wanted to risk it. He knew everyone here would have his back if he needed them to, though, and it helped him relax. Jarvis's presence helped, too, and it was a pleasure to watch him bloom.

He'd always kept himself separated. Peregrine had noticed it since the first time he'd seen him at the coffee shop, and he was glad to see that seemed to be over. Ever since Jarvis had faced his mother, something had loosened inside of him, and even though he was still awkward sometimes, he was more than happy to chat with Sam and Toby. It wouldn't have happened a few weeks ago, and Peregrine knew that his presence in Jarvis's life was partly responsible for it. The other part was all Jarvis, though, and Peregrine loved him all the more for that.

The two of them stayed around the fire pit for most of the evening. It looked like everyone wanted to talk to Peregrine, but he was more than happy to take a step back and allow Jarvis to take charge of the conversations. Jarvis looked bewildered a few times, but then he seemed to understand that this was a lot for Peregrine. It was a lot for him, too, but he'd grown up with these people, so he knew how to deal with them.

Peregrine even managed to slip away after a while. He needed to use the bathroom, so he headed toward Cam and Toby's house. He was relieved when the front door closed behind him. He took a moment to breathe in and out in the darkness of the entrance.

This was what the rest of his life could be like if he stayed. He'd be part of the pack, and no one would find him out of place at a cookout. The pack would eventually get used to seeing him around, and they would stop watching him like he was an animal at the zoo. It would take time, and it would be uncomfortable since Peregrine wasn't used to it, but he thought he could do it for Jarvis — and for himself.

Because all of this was giving him a chance to have a real life — a life he'd only been able to dream about until now, and he wanted it. He could imagine himself staying, being with Jarvis, and eventually, building a family with him. He could imagine himself still being here when he was old and his hair was white rather than blond.

He shook his head. Those were dreams, and they wouldn't happen if they didn't find a way to protect him from the people after him. Right now, if he could, he would gladly give away his ability to heal if it meant being left in peace. Unfortunately, there wasn't a way to make it happen, so he pushed that thought away and headed to the bathroom.

A crash in the kitchen made him freeze as he was on his way out of the house again. He turned around, wondering if Toby or Cam had dropped something and needed help. He could hear hushed voices, and he hoped it wasn't someone who shouldn't be here. He wouldn't be surprised if that was the case. Toby and Cam were very open to the pack, which meant that anyone could come into their house when they wanted to. Peregrine didn't understand it, but then, he wasn't the alpha or the alpha mate.

He walked toward the kitchen, ready to help if someone needed him. He should have been more careful. He should have remembered that someone was hunting him.

When he stepped into the kitchen, he realized his mistake as soon as he saw the two men standing by the back door. He knew they weren't part of the pack. They were dressed all in black, their faces covered, and a plate was in pieces by their feet. They both looked at him when they heard him, and the three of them froze for a few seconds.

Then one of them raised the mask he was wearing, and Peregrine recognized the man from the motel. He took a step back in the hallway, but the man raised the gun he was holding. "I wouldn't do that if I were you," he whispered.

The other guy stepped forward. "If you don't want your friends out there to get hurt, you'll come with us. Don't start screaming, and don't try to run. We won't hesitate to shoot all of them if you refuse to come with us."

Peregrine couldn't breathe. Before, he would have shifted and flown away. He couldn't do that in this situation. Jarvis was out there, along with other people Peregrine cared about. He couldn't put any of them in danger, but especially not

Jarvis. He would never forgive himself if anything happened to him.

He'd been found. He wasn't sure how these two guys had managed to find a way inside Cam's house, but he supposed it had something to do with the cookout. With everyone gathered around the pit, it would have been easy for them to sneak into pack territory and get to the house. Peregrine shouldn't have gone anywhere on his own, but he'd thought going to the bathroom was safe.

He'd been wrong.

Someone was bound to notice what was happening, and he didn't want that to happen. He especially didn't want Jarvis to come looking for him while these two guys were in the house. That meant he had to go with them willingly.

They wouldn't kill him. He was too valuable, which was why they were after him. That didn't mean Jarvis or the pack would be able to find him if he left, unfortunately. He had no way to know, but he also had no choice. The only thing he could do was move toward the man and let them do what they wanted with him.

Jarvis held his breath. Peregrine had whispered he was going to the bathroom a while ago, and Jarvis had lost track of time. It had been too long for Peregrine to still be inside the house. That was why Jarvis had followed him inside, wondering if he and Peregrine could steal a moment alone. They wouldn't have sex anywhere in Cam's house, but that didn't mean they couldn't just hug each other and have a bit of quiet time.

Then Jarvis had heard the voices.

At first he'd thought Peregrine was talking to Toby or Cam. It would make sense, since this was their house, but Jarvis had seen them outside, which meant it was someone else. He'd been cautious as he walked toward the kitchen, and he'd made sure whoever was inside couldn't see him.

Now he was grateful he'd done all of that. He listened as Peregrine promised he wouldn't try anything, and he knew he had to intervene. These two men would take Peregrine away, and Jarvis would never see him again. The thought of that made him feel like he was suffocating, and while he knew Peregrine wouldn't want him to sacrifice himself, he was ready to do just that if it meant Peregrine would be free.

They'd both been idiots. They shouldn't have come to the cookout, and Jarvis knew Peregrine had been worried. Jarvis had wanted him to see how many people in the pack cared about him and that he was truly one of them now. He'd wanted to show him that he would be missed if he left, and he'd believed this was the best way to do that.

But instead, he'd put Peregrine in danger. These people had found him, and they would take him away. Jarvis couldn't allow that to happen.

"Tie him up," one of them ordered.

"He's not going to run. You heard him," the other said.

"You want to risk it? What do you think will happen if he runs and his people find out we're here?"

"We shoot them."

"There are dozens of people outside, dumbass. You wouldn't be able to kill all of them, and you'd have the rest after you. Don't be an idiot—tie him up."

Jarvis quietly toed his shoes off. Then he pushed his jeans past his legs and pulled his t-shirt off. His underwear was next, but he didn't bother with the socks. He shifted and shook his back legs, dropping the socks onto the floor with the rest of his clothes.

He crouched and moved toward the kitchen door. He could hear that the two guys were still in there, no doubt tying up Peregrine. Jarvis had to get to them before they could get Peregrine out and away from the pack, but he also didn't want to jump in without at least seeing what was going on.

He peeked inside. Two men dressed in black were standing by the back door. Peregrine was with them, his hands held out, and one of the men was tying his wrist together with a plastic strip. The other — the one from the motel — was looking around, but he didn't see Jarvis. Jarvis was thankful for that, since both of them had guns.

Jarvis swallowed. There was a good chance he would get hurt if he tried anything — but that wouldn't be enough to stop him. Nothing would. He was terrified he'd get shot but even more scared that Peregrine would.

The best thing to do would be to go back and get someone, but there wasn't time. The guy from the motel turned and opened the back door, and Jarvis knew he had to act. He took a deep breath, then another, and he jumped into the kitchen.

It took him only a few seconds to land on the guy who was opening the door. He jostled Peregrine to the side as he did so, and he heard him cry out. He couldn't stop to make sure Peregrine was okay, no matter how much he wanted to.

The guy's head cracked when he landed on the floor with Jarvis on top of him. Jarvis was ready to bite the man's throat like he'd done to the one in the motel, but before he could, something heavy landed against his side. He hit the table, pushing it across the room. The plates and glasses that had been on it dropped to the floor, making a ruckus. Jarvis hoped it meant someone would hear it, but he couldn't count on it, not with the noise outside.

He got to his feet, but he was attacked before he could do anything. One of the men had shifted into a tiger, and he was much bigger than Jarvis. Jarvis's mouth was dry, but he tried to ignore the fear. He jumped at the tiger, but the beast was expecting it. He moved to the side and raked his nails along Jarvis's side.

Jarvis yelped, and his world exploded in pain. He'd never

fought with anyone, and he had no idea where to start. He'd been lucky at the motel, but it looked like he wouldn't be this time.

He dropped to the floor. He could feel the blood dripping from his side, but he needed Peregrine to be okay. Hopefully, Peregrine had shifted and left, but when Jarvis looked up, he found Peregrine kneeling next to him, reaching for his side. Jarvis opened his mouth to tell him to go, but one of the men—the one who hadn't shifted, the one from the motel— grabbed Peregrine's arm and tried to pull him to his feet.

Peregrine twisted around and hit the guy with both his hands, since they were still tied together. The guy stumbled back, and Jarvis could have cried when a hand landed on the man's shoulder and he caught fire.

Help had arrived.

Jarvis closed his eyes. He was getting cold, and he was losing a lot of blood. He didn't think he would make it, but he didn't regret it. He would do it again if it meant saving Peregrine.

"Can't you do that outside?" someone grumbled.

Jarvis opened his eyes and almost laughed at the look on Carey's face. What had once been a man was reduced to a small pile of ashes on the floor. Jarvis had no idea how it could have happened, but he could feel the heat still coming from it.

"What was I supposed to do? He was going to take Peregrine away," Carey said.

"You didn't have to do it in my kitchen," Toby grumped.

Something soft touched Jarvis's face, and he blinked at it. He hadn't seen Peregrine shift, and his eyes widened when he realized what Peregrine was about to do. The white bird had settled on his chest, and Peregrine was staring at him.

Jarvis shook his head and tried to shift, but it hurt too much. Peregrine glared—Jarvis hadn't realized it was possible in that form, and if he hadn't been wounded, he would be laughing in Peregrine's face, because it was hilarious to see a bird glare.

"You don't have to do this," Toby said. He knelt next to Jarvis and looked at Peregrine. "Sam is coming, and we'll heal him. You don't have to take away the pain this time."

Peregrine continued glaring, although now it was directed toward Toby. Jarvis could almost hear what Peregrine was thinking.

The people after him already knew where he was. He had no intention of leaving, so why *shouldn't* he take the pain away from Jarvis?

Jarvis wanted to tell him it wasn't worth it, but when Toby and Sam started healing him, he was grateful for the small weight of Peregrine on his chest. It hurt almost as much as being wounded had, but once again, he wasn't sorry. He'd been ready to lose his life to save Peregrine, and while he hoped he would never have to do anything like this again, no one could promise him that.

That was okay. He would fight for Peregrine for as long as Peregrine needed him to.

CHAPTER SEVEN

Peregrine couldn't look away from Jarvis, even after a few hours had passed. He didn't regret taking away Jarvis's pain a second time. Hell, if he had to, he would take it away a third, fourth, and so on. For as long as he was with Jarvis, Jarvis wouldn't have to feel pain when he was hurt. Peregrine only wished there was more he could do for him, but thankfully, Sam and Toby had been there.

The entire pack had been there. Peregrine had been surprised by how angry they'd been that Jarvis had been hurt, but maybe he shouldn't have been. Even though Jarvis was a loner, he was still part of the pack. He was one of them, and he was theirs to protect.

Peregrine was worried that someone had managed to get into pack territory. It no doubt had been because of the cookout, but he couldn't ask the pack to stop living their lives just because he was in danger. He was still thinking about leaving, but one glare from Toby had been enough to keep him where he was by Jarvis's side. Even now, sitting in Cam's office, he had no intention of going anywhere. Even though it would be for the best, he couldn't find it in himself to leave Jarvis and everything else behind.

"I'm sorry you had to go through this again," Cam told Jarvis.

Jarvis was still a bit pale, but Toby and Sam had promised he was completely healed. He'd lost some blood, which was why he was sipping some juice and eating a cookie, but he would be fine. Peregrine had thought he'd lost him when he

saw the tiger shifter wound him. He'd been angry and ready
to do anything he had to do to protect Jarvis, but thankfully,
the others had arrived, and Peregrine had been able to focus
on Jarvis.

One of the men who'd attacked was dead. He was a pile of
ash that Carey had vacuumed away before Toby yelled at him
that it had been a person and that even though they'd tried to
kidnap Peregrine, they deserved better than being vacuumed.
Carey had pouted, and Peregrine wasn't sure if he was more
amused or horrified by the situation. He would never be
bored if he stayed with the pack, that was for sure.

The other man had been wounded, but he would be fine.
Cam had locked him away in one of the guest bedrooms in
his house, making Peregrine and probably everyone else uncomfortable. Cam wasn't sure what to do with the guy, which
was why they were in his office right now.

"You should let the healer see you," Cam murmured,
watching Peregrine.

Peregrine had clearly missed part of the conversation.
Cam, Jarvis, Toby, and Griffin, Cam's beta, were all staring at
him.

He cleared his throat. "I don't need to see the healer. I'm
fine. The only one who was wounded was Jarvis, and Sam
and Toby took care of him."

Cam stared at Peregrine for a moment longer before nodding. "All right. Just remember that if you need anything, you
only have to ask. I'm sorry for what happened to you."

Peregrine could see Cam felt guilty, and he didn't want
him to. "Don't worry about it."

Toby snorted. "How can we not? You're under our protection, and you almost got kidnapped. You would have been if
Jarvis hadn't been there for you."

"You and the pack can't stop living just because I'm in danger. I'm used to being in this kind of situation, and while I

can't say I enjoy it, I can deal with it. Don't worry about me, at least not when it comes to this."

Cam nodded and turned his attention to Griffin. "What do you think?"

Griffin sighed. "That we don't have a choice anymore. There are too few of us, even with Lennox and Carey. They can't be everywhere at once, and they can't protect the entire pack. We could assign them to Peregrine, but that would leave Sam and Toby exposed."

Peregrine opened his mouth to offer to leave, but Jarvis squeezed his hand, and when Peregrine turned to look at him, he was glaring. Peregrine could tell he was silently daring him to say something like what he'd been thinking of saying, and he pressed his lips together.

Jarvis was right. Peregrine was done running, and that meant he had to face the situation head-on. There would always be someone coming after him, but if he and the pack could find a way to deal with it, he would be safe, and so would the pack.

That was what he wanted. He'd never wished to settle down, or rather, he'd never allowed himself to think about doing it. It hadn't been possible until he'd met the pack. Now it was, but it would take some sacrifice and a lot of effort both from him and the pack. The fact that they were willing to do it was incredible, and Peregrine didn't want to ignore that sacrifice.

"What will we do?" he asked.

Cam looked satisfied that he'd included himself in the decision. "Griffin and I have been talking. There's a pack close by."

"It's not the Springfield pack, is it?" Jarvis asked.

Cam shook his head. "It's not. I wouldn't trust them with my dirty laundry."

Peregrine hadn't been in Rosewood long, but he knew

about the Springfield pack and what they'd done. It might have been only a few people in the pack, but it had been enough to break what little trust there had been between their pack and Rosewood. He was grateful they wouldn't have to rely on those people, because he didn't think he could trust them, either.

"We're talking about the Wakefield pack," Griffin intervened. "The old alpha and Cam's father didn't get along, but they both passed away."

"I haven't contacted them yet," Cam continued. "But I've heard good things about the new alpha, and they're much bigger than we are. They can offer protection, and I think it would be the easiest way to deal with the situation. Of course, there's no guarantee the new alpha would even want to talk to me, but if Peregrine agrees, I'm going to try."

Peregrine frowned. "What would it mean? What would they demand from you to agree to help us?"

"I don't know. I don't have a way to find out until I talk to them. If you're okay with this solution, I'll contact them tomorrow and see what happens."

"And if they refuse to help?"

Cam grimaced. "Then we're back to square one. You and Jarvis will have to go back to the safe house either way, but if Wakefield agrees to help us, we might eventually find a way to keep you safe. I don't know how yet, and I can't make promises, unfortunately."

Peregrine flopped against the back of his chair. "That's fine." And it was.

He didn't care where he had to stay or how long he had to hide as long as Jarvis was safe and they could be together. Right now, hiding in the safe house felt like the best thing they could do, and Peregrine yearned for the peace he and Jarvis had found there. As happy as he'd been to be invited to the cookout, he wished they hadn't come. None of this would have happened.

But then, Jarvis wouldn't have talked to his brother. Not everything that had happened tonight was bad, and Peregrine had to keep that in mind. He also had to keep in mind that the pack truly considered him one of them. He hadn't quite believed it until now, but he could see how convinced the people in the office were. They weren't the only ones, either. After Jarvis had been healed, a lot of people had filed into the kitchen, wanting to check in on him and Peregrine and reassuring Peregrine they would keep an eye out for him.

Jarvis's mother was probably the only one who didn't care if Peregrine lived or died, but Peregrine couldn't have cared less. Eventually, the two of them would have to have a chat and find a way to at least tolerate each other for Jarvis's sake, but for now, Peregrine wasn't planning on it. He wanted to stay as far away from her as he could, and going back to the safe house would make that happen.

She'd been understandably scared for Jarvis when she'd found out he'd been hurt, and she'd tried to use it as a way to force him back home. Thankfully, Toby and Sam had healed him, and he'd stood up to her until the only thing she could do was leave. Peregrine had been relieved to see the back of her.

"I'm sorry," Jarvis murmured.

Peregrine leaned closer to him. Cam, Toby, and Griffin were talking about the Wakefield pack and the new alpha, so he and Jarvis could have a few moments together. "What are you sorry about? You saved me again. If anything, *I'm* sorry. You shouldn't have to do anything like that, and I hate that you were hurt because of me."

Jarvis shook his head. "I didn't get hurt because of you. I got hurt because someone tried to kidnap you, and that guy decided to try to kill me. You can't take that responsibility on your shoulders because you had nothing to do with it."

"I love you." The words were out before Peregrine could stop them, and he was glad. He'd never told Jarvis, but Jarvis needed to know.

Jarvis's eyes widened. "Really?"

"You can't tell me you didn't suspect I had feelings for you. Besides, I told you I liked you." And they were mates, but that wasn't enough to create feelings. It wasn't the reason Peregrine loved Jarvis.

Jarvis shrugged one shoulder. "You did, but I didn't think you could really love me."

"Why not? You're everything I could ever want from a mate."

Jarvis licked his lips. "I'm just so ordinary."

"But you're not. I wouldn't change anything about you, even if I could. But I don't have to, because you're not ordinary, Jarvis. You're everything, and I hope that one day, you'll see yourself the way I see you." And Peregrine would try his best to *make* Jarvis see.

He wasn't going anywhere. He'd found a home, and it was thanks to Jarvis. Peregrine was finally done running, and he wouldn't have it any other way.

About the Author

Catherine is the creator of several series, most of them paranormal, including the Whitedell Pride Series and the Gillham Pack Series. While she graduated in translation, she decided to go the writer's way because it was more fun to create her own stories and characters.

She's been living in Italy for more than twenty years, but she's a daughter of the North—Belgium to be precise—and she misses it so much that she's already planning to move back.

She loves pizza—probably too much—her son, her pets, and of course, books. She sneaks some reading time into her schedule every time she has five minutes free from writing, demands from her various pets and son, and lastly, housework.

Connect with her:

lievens.catherine@gmail.com
BookBub: https://www.bookbub.com/authors/catherine-lievens
Website: https://authorcatherinelievens.com/
Facebook: https://www.facebook.com/catherine.lievens.9
Facebook Group: https://www.facebook.com/groups/411788002341528/
Twitter: https://twitter.com/authorCLievens
Newsletter: http://eepurl.com/c-uvKn